Katie ∾ *An Impertinent Fairy Tale*

By B. J. Chute

The Fields Are White
The End of Loving
Greenwillow
The Blue Cup and Other Stories
The Moon and the Thorn
One Touch of Nature and Other Stories
The Story of a Small Life
Katie: An Impertinent Fairy Tale

Katie

An Impertinent Fairy Tale

by B. J. Chute

E. P. Dutton / New York

Library of Congress Cataloging in Publication Data
Chute, Beatrice Joy
    Katie : an impertinent fairy tale.
    I. Title.
PZ3.C475Kat [PS3505.H99]   813'.5'2   77-11658
ISBN: 0-525-13826-9

Published simultaneously in Canada by Clarke, Irwin &
Company Limited, Toronto and Vancouver

Designed by Ann Gold

10 9 8 7 6 5 4 3 2 1

First Edition

for my two dear sisters

Katie ∾ *An Impertinent Fairy Tale*

Prologue ≈

Once upon a time, there were four daughters. They all had the same mother, but they all had different fathers.

For the sake of convenience, they shared the surname of Thorne, retrieved by Mama's memory from a street somewhere in Rhode Island (although it may have been Maryland), which was the scene of her first elopement. As a family name, Thorne appealed to her; it was aristocratic, but solid, an ancestral brick wall sheltering her garden of pretty byblows.

And pretty they were, as uniquely themselves as their Christian, though not Christian-at-a-font, names. They were as different from each other as their random fathers, and yet as like each other as their distracting mother, who

I

could not be seen by a man but he at once wanted to sweep her off her feet in her own best interests.

In a more conventional household, this quality of Mama's might have presented a problem, but for Mama herself, for Clovelly, Dawn, and Octavia, there was no problem at all. For Katie, the youngest, there was. Katie believed in marriage.

One ∾

It was a house of petticoat rule. With occasional selective excep-
tions, the gentlemen in it were merely boarders.

The one constant exception was Mr. Cornelius Porter,
one of the three bank presidents in Falling Grove, a small
American town founded by Mr. Porter's great-uncle,
whose own great-great-uncle had had the foresight to build
his first home on top of an oil well in far-off Texas. In the
course of many decades, Falling Grove expanded and almost became a small American city, and Cornelius Porter
himself was mentioned as a likely candidate for Governor
of the State. Nothing whatever came of the mention, but
the glow lingered, and the Superior Bank of Falling Grove
owned by its most prominent citizen became, in its small
American way, the leading bank.

Cornelius Porter was a genial banker and a genial man. His wife, who was somewhat larger than a mouse but less aggressive, had borne him first a boy, then a girl, then a pair of twins (assorted). Mrs. Porter loved her children, her garden, and her husband, in that order, and all she really asked of life was to be let alone. The children eventually grew up and left home, the garden prospered, and the arrival of Mrs. Thorne relieved Mrs. Porter from any sense of marital responsibility. Mr. Porter was occasionally an unbridled man, and, try as she might, his spouse was never quite able to conceal her dismayed feeling that she was being cornered.

The arrival of Mama, therefore, was in the nature of a blessing. When Cornelius announced at the dinner table that he had arranged to set up an unfortunate little widowed lady named Thorne, burdened by four growing girls, in a small boarding house on the outskirts of Falling Grove, and that he certainly regarded this as a sound banking investment, Mrs. Porter understood at once. She had been hoping for something of the sort, without quite putting it into thoughts, and the reports that eventually came back to her from her closest friends (who, of course, thought it no less than their duty) were most reassuring as to the widowed lady's charms and availability. Mrs. Porter hummed in her garden, went to bed at whatever hour she wanted to without fear of seeming inviting, and became the very embodiment of womanly inattentiveness.

As to Cornelius Porter's claim of a sound banking investment, this was almost credible. Some years earlier, the Superior Bank had taken reluctant title to a large and tired old house, which had been built, foolishly, as a gaming house in a part of the country where no one wanted to gamble legally. The builder, who was too crooked to be

4

really competent and did everything the hard way, sold the house at a dispiriting loss, and vanished. Subsequent buyers sank, one by one, into similar financial bogs. The town of Falling Grove grew stubbornly in the opposite direction, mortgages overlapped the roof like shingles, and a hornet's nest of exceptional size clogged the back door.

It was a hopeless house, in need of a responsible mistress. Cornelius's needs were not so different, and a transfer of the property was easily concluded, with two signatures and an Affidavit of Trust in lieu of cash. Mama wept on her banker's shoulder and dried her tears on the linen handkerchief which she abstracted, very touchingly, from his breast pocket. When she returned it to him later, it had been ironed by Clovelly, who had an indolent gift for making things look exquisitely neat on the surface.

Clovelly was Mama's firstborn, the flowering of that Maryland elopement (although it may have been Rhode Island), a tawny chrysanthemum of a girl with gold eyes, a wide mouth, and a disposition like thick sweet honey. Clovelly's contribution to the household economy was that she took in laundry—a shirt here, a necktie there—and could mend anything that broke, on which occasions her indolence left her and she whistled through her teeth like a boy. The gentlemen boarders eagerly offered their expert aid, but she liked to be alone with the toughness of tools and the resistance of solid wood and metal, and she would have been very happy as a garage mechanic. No matter; she was happy anyway.

As for Dawn, the second daughter, she had come two years behind Clovelly, fathered by a thin gypsy of a man who never stayed in one place any longer than a running silver ball of mercury and who had paid Mama the compliment of staying in one place for the better part of six months. By the time he left her, Mama was getting a little bored as he was constantly pointing at sunsets and quoting his own poems about whales and archangels, which he wrote in small notebooks and some of which bore more than an accidental resemblance to William Blake. (Mama had never heard of William Blake, and, as far as she was concerned, sunsets were best observed through a window.) Dawn had inherited neither her father's literary tastes nor his wanderlust, but her turn of mind was such that she might have been conceived in a briar patch and born in a wildwood, which she certainly was not. She had a real need to be outdoors and managed to spend most of her time among leaves and wings and rocks and all the natural objects which her mother, rather singularly, referred to as "the brute creation." She was as thin a gypsy as her father, with a tangle of brown hair and an eye sharp as a shooting star, and she could be very prickly. Once, she had pushed a large and handsome salesman out of the house in the middle of the night (he was a twice-a-year man, travelling in fine soaps and lotions), simply because he had called her a delicious creature and persisted in doing so even when the delicious creature bit him. Since he could not believe that he himself was not equally delicious, he never returned to Dawn's good graces and spent subsequent visits to Falling Grove in the doldrums of its finest hotel, palms in the lobby and dust under the bed. It was an odd business altogether, and Mama, Clovelly and Octavia never really understood it, although Octavia almost did, being from time to time somewhat prickly herself.

In Octavia's case, you could not properly trace this fault to her father. He was as unbuttoned a man as one could ask for, jovial and uncalculating and a great joy to Mama, who found living with him rather like living with a street carnival. As a baby, Octavia was placid, firm, and pleasing to look upon. At nineteen, she was placid, firm, and extremely beautiful, with an arched foot, a swan's throat, and dark brows over summer eyes. She could cook like an angel when she chose, but, like an angel, she was unconventional in her ways. Whipped puddings, winy sauces, delicacies of the most floating perfection, had been known to turn up at the boarders' breakfasts, accompanied by thrifty oatmeal that was as lumpy as a marsh.

It was Katharina who could make oatmeal that was not only lumpless but robust—Katharina, who had been called Katie from the moment she opened green eyes on a white world in the middle of a March snowstorm.

Katie's paternity was never altogether clear, as, at the time, Mama had been travelling rather merrily around the country with her three beautiful little girls and experiencing a whole series of very amiable encounters. Katie's birth was the only one at which Mama had achieved a really stately lying-in, though one forgets exactly why, and, when Katie first saw her trio of half-sisters, they were lined up ceremoniously at the foot of Mama's bed, vaguely awed by the hospital nuns who seemed to move on tiny wheels under their pale robes and who kept pushing the children's hair back from their foreheads with firm, rough hands.

Octavia said, "Oh, she's a very nice baby, Mama," with the relief of one who has waited nine months and almost given up hope, and then she addressed herself to the baby and said "Katharina" to confirm kinship with the small thing.

"Katie," said Mama, turning back a corner of the soft blue blanket to give her nestling a wider horizon.

Octavia said, "Katie, then," unprotestingly, but Clovelly's brow clouded. It was Clovelly who had chosen the new baby's name. Mama shot her a look of quick sympathy and murmured something under her breath about the Mother Superior being Irish. Clovelly, who had no idea what a Mother Superior might be, was clever enough to know that Mama was somehow indebted to the softly wheeling nuns, and so she held her peace, and Katie became Katie forever.

In one way, the name fitted her, and in one way it didn't. She was Katie all right, with those green eyes and a face like an ivory kitten, black hair down her back in a long braid, and such a shape that the Lord God (male) would have been the first to say that she was made for men's pleasure. But Katie didn't see it that way, and it took a good deal to convince the gentlemen boarders of this point of view. It puzzled them and it puzzled her family too, since some of the boarders were certainly enjoyable gentlemen, but her family was committed to total freedom of choice for both sexes. (Equality was not in question; none of them expected men to be equal.)

Katie believed in freedom of choice too, and she had nothing whatever against mating, accepting the very natural world that she lived in as a very natural world. However, for herself, mating meant lawful mating, and lawful mating meant marriage. Tracing a quirk is always a dangerous business, but it is certain that Noah was an early influence.

Of all the stories Katie had ever heard, Noah's was the best, and she had heard it first from Dawn, who was a very good storyteller. Dawn favored Noah because he had invited so many animals into his Ark, all trooping in under that one roof—the fowls after their kind, and the cattle after their kind, and every creeping thing after his kind—and it also pleased Dawn that the real heroine of the tale was a dove. Katie was pleased about the dove, too, but what she really liked best was the symmetry of that methodical embarkation, everything male and female, everything two by two.

"It doesn't mean they were *married*," Mama had pointed out, trying to get some sense of decorum into the head of her youngest. Katie replied that Noah was married, and so was his wife, and so were all his sons, and so were his sons' wives, and that was how they were supposed to be, two by two, for life. Noah had arranged it that way, and, if Dawn had her heroine dove, Katie had her hero Noah. Dawn said, tolerantly, "Katie likes things to be tidy." Mama said it was probably having been born in a Catholic hospital, you never knew what the dear Sisters were saying. Clovelly said, "She'll grow out of it," and Octavia smiled her placid smile.

But Katie did not grow out of it. At an early age, she had promised herself a lawful husband. A two-by-two world, if not an Ark, lay securely in Katie's future, and she was content to wait.

9

Two &

There were bound to be children dropping by constantly, not only the raggle-taggle ones who had nowhere to go after school, if they went to school at all, but also the prosperous ones who were expected to get home promptly. The Thornes, all five of them, exerted a terrible fascination over the young of Falling Grove; the house was a place where they could always get attention from somebody, and where nobody warned them to wipe their feet. If they tracked mud on the floors, they knew perfectly well where to find the mopping-up rag; if they forgot, the faintest turn of Clovelly's wrist seemed to remind them. Sometimes, the more anxious young insisted on cleaning on and on, halfway up the staircase, in an act of propitiation to their parents who would surely be proud to see them so hard at work, so zealous and so scrupulous.

The passage of time, eventually, did its wholesome work, and the parents asked fewer questions. An occasional flurry of morality might drift across a shop counter, a bridge table, a back fence, or even a Sunday roast, but the talk never went very far, since the spiderweb thread of inquiry always seemed to lead to such awkward flies, not to mention such prominent citizens. After all, "that place," as it was so felicitously described, was beyond the town limits, and some day a nightmare or a strong wind might topple the feeble house into another county altogether. Mama's boarders were all good spenders in town, and, as for Mama and her brood, there were many who regarded them as an architectural community asset. Uncommonly friendly, too.

It was true there were occasional misunderstandings among the male citizenry, but these always seemed to relate to Katie. It was not that the youngest of the Thornes was unsociable, she was not even censorious, but she did contrive to keep her distance in a manner that could be maddeningly effective. Pattable as a kitten, she was like a kitten in being agile, so that straying hands found themselves patting air, while Katie, distance, and a sweet smile calmed the gallop of a hopeful heart. However, these disarmed gentlemen seldom felt diminished, and some even succeeded in convincing themselves that it was they who had been gallant, rather than she who had been cavalier. Unlike Dawn, Katie had never been known to bite.

It must, therefore, have been a feeling of early summer in the air that precipitated the incident which finally set Mama (after she had thought about it for a while) to fretting seriously over her lastborn.

It was a slack time in the travelling season, and mornings were leisurely. In fact, there were only three boarders in the house that day—two at the breakfast table, and the third upstairs with Octavia, who was an old and cherished friend. Dawn was off somewhere with the moonset or the sunrise, Clovelly was polishing her long rose-pale fingernails on a napkin and humming lightly, and Mama was filling Mr. Hermitage's cup so full of coffee that there would be no room for sugar. She had several little economies of this kind, all of them founded on the theory that, if one were truly thrifty in small ways, one could make up for it in large ways, such as extravagance.

Mr. Hermitage, a lank man with a tidy moustache and dormant sideburns, had been thirty years with the firm of Oakes & Peppard, and he considered himself well enough established in the Thorne household to offer a pat on the small plump hand that now extended the steaming cup. He was rewarded with a smile of such surpassing sweetness (something about the sideburns had reminded Mama of a long-ago pair of them, tender and blond) that his heart and his cup leaped together. Half the cup's contents slopped onto the tablecloth, laid fresh that very morning.

Mama murmured in dismay and sympathy. Katie sprang to mop up, not only the tablecloth but also Mr. Hermitage's damp knees, which had fortunately escaped most of the deluge. The soft round warmth of her brushed against him, but he only said an autumnal "Thank you, my dear." It was the very young boarder, seated at his right, who overreached himself. Catching Katie around the slender waist that was so close to hand, he tried frolicsomely to pull her down onto his lap. She spun away, her hands flew wide, and somehow, in the next moment, it was his bowl of oatmeal and not Katie which landed upside down on the young boarder's lap.

He gave a lonely yelp, like a puppy stepped on. "Oh, dear me!" said Katie brightly, bestowed one more housewifely swipe to the Hermitage knees, and then handed her cloth to the latest victim.

He took the cloth, put his head down, and began to scrub at his trousers. The oatmeal, this morning, was Octavia's creation, adhesive and soggy, and it was of no benefit to his only suit. He felt confusion and sorrow.

"Poor, dear man," said Mama, casting a look of faint reproach at her daughter. Katie's look in turn was very serene, but, after a moment, she dropped her eyes and bit her lip.

"They'll need sponging," Clovelly observed, added unexpectedly, "I'll do them," and held out her hand.

"It was my fault, I'll do them," Katie said without enthusiasm, and held out her hand too.

The young man, surrounded by conflicting claims on his trousers, ducked his head even lower and scrubbed even harder. Mr. Hermitage, coffee on his own trousers more than compensated for by oatmeal on another's, said cheerfully, "Take 'em off, my boy." Clovelly gave a small laugh, a miniature sound, meaning nothing at all. Mama's echo was more in the nature of a chime, meaning even less.

The young man's ears, already pink, began to glow like rubies. He had no idea what to do, and the oatmeal was as perverse as the company with its unfortunate sense of humor. Miserably, he raised his nose; it too was pink.

Katie took pity. "Take your trousers off in the kitchen," she told him, "and go up the back stairs. I'll leave them outside your door."

"Th-thank you," said the young man, and fled the scene, narrowly missing Dawn, who had wandered in from without by the back door. She gazed after him tranquilly, dropped a wholly unmotivated kiss on the top of Mr. Hermitage's head, and slid into the vacated seat. "Be careful of the oatmeal," Mama warned. "Katie threw it at Arthur."

"I did not," said Katie.

"Pet, you did," Mama said, added, "He'll be out of his trousers by now," and reached to refill Mr. Hermitage's cup, this time donating a generous spoonful of sugar, simply because the blessing of Dawn's kiss had made him look so suddenly young.

"No sugar, Mrs. Thorne," said Mr. Hermitage, too late.

Murmuring at her forgetfulness, Mama curved both hands around his cup, inhaled the dark sweet brew, and began to sip it meditatively. Katie paused on her way to the kitchen, filled another cup, without sugar, and set it trimly in front of Mr. Hermitage. He leaned back and inhaled the fragrance, feeling cosseted as in sunshine.

Dawn said, "It's far too warm for oatmeal anyway. Did you really throw it at Arthur, Katie?" but Katie only pressed her lips together, scooped up the oatmeal dish, and left the room with a nice whisk of her skirt.

Clovelly said, "Of course, she threw it. And very gracefully too—it almost looked like an accident."

"What happened?"

"He *presumed,*" Clovelly said demurely.

Mama sighed. The young man (his full name was Arthur Bean, but one inevitably thought of him as the young man) had arrived two days ago, and, until this morning, he had behaved so scrupulously that she had thought he might be the very person to besiege the stubborn little castle of her youngest daughter's virtue. It was Mama's pious conviction that, once Katie had dipped into the waters of Venus, she would forget all that unsuitable non-

14

sense about Noah. She sighed again (more heavily, the first sigh having gone unnoticed), and Clovelly and Dawn said, in perfect, irreverent chorus, "He's such a *sweet* young man."

"Well, he is," said Mama defensively.

"He's a mooncalf," Clovelly said, not unkindly.

Mr. Hermitage cleared his throat and observed that, in his opinion, Katie had not thrown the oatmeal, but, if she had, she was well within her rights. His own judicious thinking impressed him, and he would have amplified it, had not Mama turned her lovely eyes full upon him and said, quite truthfully, "But, my dear man, you are not a mother."

"I didn't say I was a mother," Mr. Hermitage said, aggrieved.

Clovelly interlaced her fingers, rested her chin on them, and directed her own gaze upon him, a gold-eyed pussy-cat. "You implied it," said Clovelly. "Didn't he imply it, Dawn?"

"Yes, I rather think so," said Dawn, very purely. Then, as Octavia appeared in the doorway in a ravishing dressing-gown, her gentleman friend (so agreeably ravished) beside her, Dawn said, "Didn't he, Octavia dear? Didn't Mr. Hermitage imply that he was a mother?"

Octavia knew this game of old. "Imply?" she said. "I distinctly heard him say so."

"Ah," said Mama supportively, although at her age she really should have known better.

Mr. Hermitage shook his head, not so much in the negative as to clear it of bees, and observed that he really ought to be going, he had a long hard day ahead of him. They all agreed very sweetly, making it clear they were willing to forgive his claims to motherhood; the air was as soft and as scented as talcum powder. Mr. Hermitage—knowing he did indeed have a long hard day ahead of him, knowing that he had a good wife and a fine family, knowing that he was a man of complete rectitude—Mr. Hermitage, helplessly, lingered. He did not want to stay in order to defend himself. He wanted to stay in order to be plagued by witches and to feel so young.

There was a clatter on the front stairs, and Katie flew down them and into the dining room, flushed and merry. She reached for the plate of bread, helped herself generously to butter and jelly, and began to eat.

"Did the oatmeal come off?" said Dawn.

"More or less," Katie said around the edge of her crust.

Clovelly assumed a look of mad passion and put her hands to her breast, which was heaving becomingly. "Did you give him back his trousers?" she asked throatily, and, when Katie nodded, she added, "Did he sweep you into his arms?"

Katie shook her head. "He wouldn't open his door," she said mildly, "so I hung 'em on the knob." She reached for more bread, caught Clovelly's eye, and began to laugh.

Clovelly joined her, then Dawn—two flute sounds with Mama's piccolo giggle following them. Mr. Hermitage and Octavia's gentleman friend sat silent, not wanting to be left out but not sure how to get in, until Octavia smiled at them and released a tenor and a baritone, each of which came out, surprisingly, as a boom.

All the laughs, all on different levels, mounted the staircase and assembled themselves outside the young man Arthur's door.

He sat behind it, on the edge of the bed, his trousers dangling limply from his hand, hearing them laugh and disengaging one single laugh from all the others. He knew they were laughing at him, and his heart lay heavy inside his chest, but his fingers touched the place on his trousers—just at the knees—where *her* hand had lain. Her wet rag, anyway.

Like Mama, but for very different reasons, he sighed. The mooncalf was in love.

Three ∾

*Cornelius Porter told his wife that he would not be home for din-*ner, and she nodded placidly, accepting the words which skirted explanation and made apology unnecessary. In her way, she was very fond of Cornelius, and this fondness was translated into such things as not asking questions and putting a thermos and crackers by his bedside for nights when he might wake and find himself lonely. (He would, in some ways, have preferred to have his wife there, instead of the thermos and crackers, but she had moved out of connubiality so fleetly that he had been given no opportunity to rearrange her thoughts for her.)

Even now, as he strode down the front path between his wife's flowering borders, Mr. Porter's intellect told him that it was better so. Flourishing his cane, he flicked the head off a *Bellis perennis* named Snowflake, then impulsively reclaimed the lopped-off little sunface and held it between his fingers, stirred by a youthful impulse. She-loves-me-she-loves-me-not. Discretion prevailed, and after a moment he fastened the blossom into his buttonhole, tailoring the frail petals to the world of finance.

However, the morning was truly beautiful, and the evening, with Mrs. Thorne at its golden center, promised to be even more so. It was a slightly intoxicated banker who nodded good-day to the fat guard at the bank's grilled door, chirped a greeting to his staff, and spun his genial way into his own high-ceilinged, oak-paneled office.

A young man was sitting there, twisting his hat in his hands. The first thing that struck Mr. Porter was that the young man was almost excessively neat, except for his trousers which seemed vaguely rumpled at the knees.

The visitor leapt to his feet, fell over his well-shined shoes, dropped his hat, picked it up, smiled an anxious smile, and said, "Mr. Porter?"

There was a silence in which Cornelius hung up his own hat on his own hatrack, along with his walking stick. He then said "Yes?" in a voice which questioned the young man's very right to existence in this private office of the president of the leading bank of Falling Grove. He should never have been allowed into it at all; someone's head would have to roll. He said "Yes?" again, rolling heads.

"Sir. My name is Bean. Arthur Bean."

Cornelius sat down at his desk, pulled the morning mail to hand, and inspected it briefly. "What can I do for you?" he asked, leaving unsaid the key words, *Before I throw you out of here.*

Arthur huddled deeper into the chair, which was narrow and hard and offered a minimum of shelter. He said, speaking small so as not to disturb the air, "Stationery and supplies, sir. I represent Marcus, Welk and Hanover, very high-class items. I thought you might be interested in seeing the company's line, that is, Mrs. Thorne thought you might be interested. . . ."

Cornelius told himself that he might have known it. If the joy of his life and the light of his heart had a fault (she did), it was this tendency to send him her least competent boarders, as if they were infant chickens in need of a fiduciary hen. He thought, not for the first time, that he must warn her not to do this to him, and he knew, not for the last time, that he would do nothing of the sort. "How did you get into my office?" he demanded, and then, out of simple curiosity, "What happened to your trousers?"

"I walked in. Katie spilled oatmeal on them." He stroked his knees reverently. "She cleaned them off. I thought they looked rather well."

"Spilled?" said Cornelius incredulously, knowing Katie to be as deft as a seraph.

"Poured," Arthur amended. "Would you like to examine our samples, Mr. Porter? We handle a wide variety of . . ."

"Put me down for a gross of lined pads—" One could always use lined pads. "—and leave your catalogue with me. *Why* did Katie pour oatmeal on your trousers?"

"Letterheads in cream vellum," Arthur said, rather desperately. "Lovely inlaid writing sheets for ladies, in Breton script, which your wife would appreciate . . ."

"My wife detests writing letters," Cornelius said falsely. "Why did Katie pour oatmeal on your trousers?"

Arthur gave over licking his pencil and raised his eyes. "I offended her," he said mournfully, and added, "She's very beautiful."

Cornelius heard the bleat in the youthful voice and deduced that this young man had foolishly fallen in love with Mama's youngest. Still, who could blame the lad? and good luck to him, although it was Cornelius's opinion that the first to bed Katie would need a bit more ginger than this youngster was showing. Still, a young bleater might appeal to her maternal instinct, if any. "Well, good luck to you, young man," he said, and managed to sound almost hearty.

Arthur's sensitive ears turned pink. "You think she might . . . ?"

"Why not?"

"But she was very angry."

"It shows she cares," said Cornelius inventively. He scowled at the young idiot, who was plainly going to sit there all day licking his pencil (really, he was a blockhead), unless someone took action. "Give me your catalogue, and an order blank. I'll fill it in myself. Your hat's on the floor."

"Thank you, sir." Arthur retrieved the hat from beneath his heel, and lingered. "Excuse me, if I might ask one question—"

"Can't stop you," said Cornelius, reaching for his paperknife. The paperknife had a brass handle, overwrought with cherubs and roses, and it had been a present from his dear wife on the occasion of his ascension to the bank presidency. It was classy in a Victorian way, and he liked it very much.

"Mrs. Thorne," said Arthur, "that is, Mrs. Thorne's daughters—I have heard talk in town that . . ." He was bleating again. "I mean, it would help if I knew exactly how things stood, what I mean is . . ."

Cornelius knew exactly what he meant. "Mr. Bean," he

said, sounding a little weary, "you are far too young to be out without a guardian." He sighed. "Your hat, young man, is now in your hand. The door is behind you."

Arthur scrabbled his papers together, put his pencil back of his ear, rose and reached out across the table as if to shake Mr. Porter's hand. He then thought better of the impulse, donned his hat, knocked his pencil onto the floor, picked it up, said proudly, "I catch your meaning, sir," and headed outside.

Cornelius started to call him back, thought better of the impulse in his turn, and resigned the whole matter to Providence, in which he had a banker's natural trust. Bean, he realized, had got everything wrong, but it might be all for the best. Katie, like Providence, could look after herself.

Arthur Bean continued on his day's round, with a tempting vision of Katie dancing between him and his customers, his emotions seesawing between the beauty of her (a young man's reverence) and the certitude that she was no better than she should be (a young man's optimism). His mind occupied with such fruitful matters, he forgot everything he had ever learned about salesmanship, with the natural result that he did better than usual and returned, that evening, to Mrs. Thorne's with a bulging order book and a sense of impending conquest.

Katie and Octavia were out on the front stoop, and Octavia was reading Katie's future in a pack of worn playing cards. Had Arthur's heart not been already in Katie's net, it would have leaped like a silver fish to see Octavia, dark brows knit together over tranced eyes, the curve of her cheek shadowed by her hair. Arthur's own eyes passed over such delights and fastened upon the dimple in Katie's right elbow. Gad, thought a swaggering knight deep down inside him, that elbow shall be mine!

He remembered all the rumors he had heard in town (he had not heard the one that tied Mrs. Thorne and Mr. Porter together in a bowknot, but he would not have credited it anyway, because he esteemed banks), and he felt self-confidence swell within him. He also felt his heart pound, his pulses race, and his nerves quiver; he could hardly have been in more tiptop shape for the tournament. He cleared his throat.

A pair of blue eyes and a pair of green ones lifted gravely to meet his. In a weaker moment, he might have tumbled backwards on the grass, but he was armed with the successes of the day and with what he understood to be Mr. Porter's virile blessing. He stood his ground.

"Having a little card game?" he said. His Adam's apple bobbed, but his chin was firm. He kept from drowning in blue and green waters by shifting his gaze back to Katie's elbow.

The blue eyes dropped to the pack of cards, and Octavia purred, "No, dear boy," with her mother's precise and most trying cadence, so that he felt his trousers tighten at the knees and heard once more all those laughing voices that had drifted up the staircase that morning. He braced himself, and his trousers eased. They were lovely girls, all of them, flowers in a garden, but he knew them for what they were. Flowers in a garden are meant to be enjoyed, they are there for the plucking.

Octavia, who did not really mean to mock this dewy creature, said, "Shall I tell your fortune? I can do it without the cards."

Any salesman at Marcus, Welk & Hanover, indeed any salesman the world over, is obliged to believe in the supernatural. There are days when the Goddess of Luck hovers over them all; other days, when she leaves them to brood alone in the waste of an economic system which is poor housing for goddesses. "Please do," said Arthur graciously. "I don't believe in that kind of thing, of course."

"Of course not," Octavia agreed. Next to her, Katie drew her knees up to her chin, and wrapped her arms around them. Arthur looked down at the top of her head, hair black as midnight and just a glimpse of the tender nape of her white neck. He imagined his own voice as it murmured traditionally sweet nothings into the (traditionally) pink shell of her ear.

Octavia leaned back, gazed up into the nearest tree, and let occultism settle upon her. "Much money," she said gravely.

Arthur nodded. The day's work had foretold something of the sort.

"Many travels," said Octavia.

He nodded again, and she caught him at it and added, "Not just here and there, young man. I see distant oceans and strange grottoes and high mountains . . ."

He felt a vague dismay. Something of a homebody by nature, he had planned an early retirement from the wearying world of travelling salesmen, perhaps on that day when some bank president (college chancellor, chairman of a mighty board, Chief Justice) would offer him a modest but splendid and well-endowed alternative. He looked at Octavia doubtfully.

". . . and a beautiful wife," said Octavia.

His roving eye having just roved back to Katie, Arthur was not prepared for being endowed with a beautiful wife. An orderly portion of his mind said, *First things first,* and then, since there is nothing like a cliché to sharpen the wits, he reorganized his priorities. *Katie, first; beautiful wife, second.*

"Is that enough for the time being?" Octavia said sweetly. "Fortune. Travel. Marital bliss." She picked up the cards and ran them affectionately through her fingers, showing a rather unnerving dexterity. The bits of pasteboard flowed from palm to palm like water, and when the Ace of Diamonds leaped to her fingers and seemed to cling, Arthur felt a faint tingling along his scalp.

He gave an uncertain laugh. "You're very convincing, Miss Octavia," he said, and when she only smiled, he turned to her sister. "Katie. Come for a walk before dinner." He added, "Please," because his mother and father had both taught him to say *please* if you really wanted something.

"*Miss* Katie," said Katie, but she rose sedately and smoothed out her skirt. After a moment's hesitation, he took her hand, and she let him keep it. They moved off together, formally, a minuet of propriety. Octavia said, "So!" to the Ace of Diamonds, reinserted it into its pack of marplots, and went indoors to find her mother.

Mama had strewn herself on a sofa in a most delectable pose, managing to convey a litter of French novels and bonbons, although she actually had nothing more scandalous to convey than one of her own small shoes. It had lost its heel, and she was turning it vaguely about in her soft hands. Octavia took it away from her and said that Clovelly would mend it.

"Clovelly can mend anything," Mama said, melting the ceiling with an upward glance which she was practicing for the pleasure of Cornelius. "She gets it from her dear father. When Clovelly was born, he wanted to make a cradle for her, but I couldn't permit it, of course."

25

"Of course," Octavia agreed, and then, since this was a new story to her and she thought she had heard them all, she added, "Why not?"

"We were travelling, dear," her mother said, surprised to be asked. "One can't travel with a cradle. They were pursuing us, you know, pursuing the elopers."

Octavia said yes, she remembered that part, it was the cradle that was new. "Oh no, dear," Mama said, "I've told you about the cradle a thousand times. I made a little blue blanket for it, and it looked very sweet."

"I thought you said there wasn't any cradle."

"There wasn't," Mama said cleverly, "so I've invented the blanket too. You're looking splendid, love."

Octavia, who had had a happy night and who knew that Mama was anticipating one equally happy, nodded. They smiled at each other like old friends, then Octavia said, "Mama?"

"Octavia?"

"It's Katie, Mama. She's walking around out there with that young Bean, who's been mooning after her—She can't really see anything in him, can she?" She stuck her tongue out suddenly, flickering, like a little garden snake. "Would you want that squeeny young man for a son-in-law, Mama?"

The Widow Thorne sat up in alarm, started to say, "Katie wouldn't even dream of . . ." and then broke off. What she had been about to say was that Katie wouldn't even dream of taking the young Bean into her bed, which would certainly have been true if Katie had not held to such peculiar views on marriage. But who could tell what Katie might accept as a husband, since she thought so institutionally? Noah's Ark, with all those wedded auks and tigers!

26

"Katie's dreadfully inexperienced," Octavia said, laments in her voice. "I'm afraid she'll get herself in trouble."

"Marry someone, you mean."

"Yes. She could wreck her whole life." Wilting gracefully alongside Mama on the sofa, she added, "Mama, where does Katie get her ideas?"

"Dear, I've often wondered." Mama put both feet, one shod, one unshod, down on the floor firmly and sat admiring her ankles, which were elegant. "It may have been my fault," she murmured, after a moment of deep silence. "Her father was Catholic."

"He was?" said Octavia, as willing to pursue a religion as a cradle.

"He might have been."

"Aren't you thinking of the nuns, perhaps?"

"Well, they had to be Catholic, Octavia dear," Mama said, rather crossly. "It would have been most unsuitable if they weren't." She stopped contemplating her ankles and turned her gaze to the ceiling, which was full of interesting cracks. "I don't believe he was a Catholic, at all. If her father had been a really devout Catholic, Katie's mind wouldn't run on marriage in this strange way. She'd have taken the veil."

"Well—Suppose Arthur Bean asks her to marry him?"

"She'll refuse."

"Are you sure?" Octavia said relentlessly.

Mama put one hand to her heart and said that she would talk to Cornelius.

"Do," said Octavia, "and I'll talk to Clovelly and Dawn." She turned her head at the sound of a voice that was always comfortably welcome, and murmured, "There's Mr. Porter now." He was "Cornelius" only to his love, a

27

nice distinction which he appreciated. "Talk to him to-night, Mama, but don't spoil his dreams."

Mama looked at her reproachfully, and Octavia let her creamy eyelids drop, knowing very well how safe Mr. Porter's nights were in Mama's care.

Four ❧

"Katie," said Arthur Bean.

"Katharina," said Katie dourly.

He had led her by the hand to a discreet distance from the large-eyed windows, and when she settled herself on a grassy knoll, he dropped beside her in a troubadour attitude, propped on one elbow and his heart in his eyes. He said "Katharina" again, took the little hand which had escaped his, and pressed it tenderly.

"Yes?" said Katie, and took the little hand away.

"Nothing," said Arthur. "Just *Katharina*. It's a lovely name."

She studied him through her lashes, which were thick and soft and curled back in a such a way that she gave an impression of come and hither without necessarily intending it. She said, thank you, politely.

"Thank you, *Arthur*," he amended.

The lashes rose slowly. "Thank you, Arthur."

"Thank you, Arthur *dear*."

The lashes fell. There was a silence, and he had a sudden terrible feeling that he was boring her. He was right. Arthur's parents were nice, well-meaning people, but rather stupid, and they had not really prepared their son for lying about on the grass and gazing into eyes as green as Katie's. He felt a need to impress her. "I had an excellent day today," he said carelessly. "A great many fine orders."

"You have a natural gift?" said Katie, sounding a little like Clovelly.

He was not sure how to answer that, but he supposed she meant well. "It's not that I'm over-ambitious," he said anxiously. "That would be *bourgeois*—" He waited for her to ask him what *bourgeois* meant, but either she knew already or she didn't care, so he went on. "But I do feel capable of carving a future for myself." He had not intended to talk about his future, which would be a problem for his wife, not for Katie, but he saw a gleam in the greenness behind those curled lashes. He cleared his throat.

"You'll be rich," said Katie.

"Quite possibly." What greedy little things women were! He swelled modestly, reached for her hand and found that, this time, she let him keep it.

"It would be pleasant to be rich," Katie said. She sat there, studying him, testing him in her mind to see what he would look like, say, ten years hence—domesticated, husbandly, one-half of a connubial whole. He would perhaps be stout, since there was already a waistline curve and the hint of a second chin. He would be putty to manage, tame as a chicken. She let her hand remain in his because she felt she owed him something for his trousers, but her mind was cool as she measured him for her Ark. Nothing to dream of, thought Katie, but then she was not a dreamer.

She leaned back slightly in order to analyze his profile view, which was not memorable. A beard might help, perhaps? She was not fond of beards, but then she was not fond of Arthur either. That would come. It was a point of trust with Katie that, along with matrimony, fondness would come.

She smiled. He pressed her hand, ardently. She pressed his in return, fleetingly. Surely, this steady little man would make a steady little husband. Mama would, eventually, get used to the idea of one of her daughters marrying, knowing that the daughter's mind was so firmly set. Katie made an effort to picture Arthur through the eyes of Mama—of Octavia, of Dawn, of Clovelly. . . . She sighed uneasily and, at the sigh, Arthur's heart rose.

So did he, dusting his knees, and saying that they would be late for dinner. Whatever the state of his fortunes, Arthur always found time to think about his meals, and he was pleased when Katie rose at once to her feet and led the way home.

By the time he had washed his hands, she was already at the table. Seated next to her was Mr. Porter, who nodded affably at his morning visitor and did absolutely nothing to explain his presence in the house. Mama said, "Sit down, Arthur dear, we have a mortgage with Mr. Porter," not from any thought of explaining anything but because she found the idea of a mortgage very elevating.

Arthur, feeling so much a man of the world and understanding all, bowed to Mr. Porter, respecting even more the advice given him by that able financier. It was beautifully clear to Arthur that nothing stood in the way of prompt action.

It was after midnight when he undertook it.

Being Arthur, he had tossed for a long time on his narrow, lonely and somewhat lumpy bed. He had always found warm milk to be an antidote for restlessness, but he was now out of his home orbit. Katie, fixing herself so wilfully in his mind, was having, of course, precisely the opposite effect of warm milk, and for an hour he thrashed about in a very highstrung manner. The confident troubadour had deserted him, and he was now alone in the night with the mooncalf.

At last, he got out of bed, draped himself in his bathrobe, and began to pace—a limited occupation because the room was small. Just down the hall—and he knew precisely where—was Katie's room. He saw it in his mind's excited eye, uncertain of the furnishings but confident there would be a bed. He moved from that to seeing Katie on the bed, and, after a bit, the troubadour easily regained the upper hand.

Not pausing to think any more and breathing very rapidly, Arthur slipped out into the hallway. If he met anyone, they would assume he was going to the bathroom.

The hallway was dark, and he slid along it, counting doorknobs until he reached the fourth one. He raised his hand to knock, reconsidered, and put his nose to the edge of the door. "Katie," he said softly, waited in a long dark silence, and then said "Katharina" a little less softly. There was a draught around his ankles, because his bathrobe was too short, and he began to wonder if the whole excursion might not be a mistake.

This irritated him, and irritation bred hardihood. He lifted his hand once more, prepared to pound, if necessary, and then it occurred to him to try the doorknob. It moved easily, and he was shocked. In a houseful of male boarders, not to lock her door!

Or did he have the wrong door? Or, worse yet, was someone already in the bedroom with her?

He stood there, drenched in anxiety, his ankles chill, and his heart, a timid muscle, beating very loud. Reassuring himself that this was certainly the right door, he pulled his head together and reasoned further. If she had a boarder in there, surely the door would be locked, barred. . . . His sinews stiffened. He remembered her sigh, her hair, her eyelashes. Grasping the doorknob, he turned it boldly and pushed.

As he had foreseen, there was a bed. There was also moonlight. And there was Katie.

Her black hair spilled over the white pillow, and her green eyes were shuttered behind her white eyelids. Perversely, his heart slowed down, and he felt masterful. He strode over the threshold, closed the door behind him, and strode onward to the bed. "Katie," he announced.

She had been sleeping in perfect dreamlessness, and his voice parted endless veils. She muttered something, turned over, and buried her face in her arm. Arthur tapped the nearest curve of her possessively, and she awoke. At this point, she ought properly to have hurled herself upon him with a glad cry (wanton) or melted in shy submission (maidenly).

"Oh, for goodness' sake," she said ungraciously. "It's you."

She sat up, her nightgown slipping off one round shoulder. She pulled it up and eyed her visitor, feeling rather vexed. Following her around, she supposed. Still, if one planned to marry him, one would have to get used to that. It was the price one paid for husbands.

"Katie," said Arthur thickly, and reached for her.

She vanished. One moment, she was on the bed. The next, she had slipped through his fingers and was silhouetted against the window, with the moon caught in her hair.

Arthur stumbled after her.

"Oh, bother," Katie said.

He plunged forward, grabbing manfully, seized what ought to have been her nightgown, and gathered it into his arms. Logically, she should have been inside it, but she was not. Nor was it her nightgown that he now clutched; it was the window curtain. The phantom named Katie was across the room, and Arthur was wrapped in white dimity, fragile and cloudlike, faintly poetic.

Katie flew to rescue the curtain, which had a frill at the top, sewn by Clovelly. Arthur flailed indignantly, a windmill, and she cried out, "Arthur! Hold still!"

He held still. Behind him, there echoed the voices of generations of women telling their menfolk to hold still, leave it alone, be careful, don't bring your muddy boots into my clean kitchen. . . . A numbed cocoon, he stood and let himself be unwound, and it seemed to him, in this hour of trial, that he really did not like women very much.

"I think you've torn the frill," Katie said severely. "Take it off the rod, please, and be very careful."

He took it off the rod and he was very careful, pouring the white froth into those outstretched arms which he had earlier hoped would be outstretched in a better cause.

"Yes, you have," said Katie, examining the frill. "You've torn it quite badly."

Arthur said he had not meant to do so, which was no

34

less than God's truth. His voice was small and flat, the voice of a man who was feeling small and flat.

Katie, who did not like meekness, shrugged, wandered off to collect needle and thread, and then came back to sit crosslegged on the bed. C863068 co. schools

Arthur gazed at her, drift of dimity on her lap, moon on her hair, toes curling and uncurling at the hem of her nightgown. "Do you *want* me to go?" said Arthur, trying to pack all the possible responses into one question mark.

"No, no," Katie murmured. "The damage is done, you can stay while I mend the poor thing. Sit down, do."

He sat down, but, on the basis of her promising words, he felt much less meek. Sewing the curtain was, plainly, no more than a ruse to keep him there, and, from a young man who had just done grievous wrong to a curtain, he became once more a young man alone in a boudoir with his intended light of love. Three paces, he calculated, would take him to her side. He had only to put his hands on those white shoulders, and she would fall backwards. . . .

Katie bit off a length of thread, set her needle and began to sew, earnestly, with large stitches that had a sort of rocking-horse regularity. As she sewed, she too calculated. Naturally, it was perfectly obvious to Mama's daughter why Arthur had come barging into her room, in the middle of the night, knees quaking and eyes as big and bold as a frog's. It was nothing to hold against a man, but, on the other hand, it was not the kind of approach that led to the altar, which was where Katie intended to go. Arthur Bean's plans for the night would have to be rearranged.

She gave him a quick glance, as green as April, and he lurched to his feet.

35

"Would you hold the other end of the curtain up for me?" Katie said demurely.

He was on his feet, anyway. It would be uncivil to refuse. He accepted his share of white dimity with reluctance and stood holding it, stiff as a hitching post, while Katie scanned its length for further damage. "It'll do now, I think," she said at last.

He cast it to the ground—not an easy gesture with something so clinging. Katie said, "Be careful," her voice like a cool hand on a fevered brow. Then she looked up, smiled gravely, and added, "Just a few more stitches, perhaps."

He sat down again.

She bent her head to her work and continued her calculations. Not the ideal husband, of course, but conceivable. Harmless, certainly; intelligent, perhaps. Clovelly had called him a mooncalf, but she had meant it kindly, and, anyway, Clovelly would never favor anything that fitted into Noah's Ark. The fowls after their kind, and the creeping things after their kind, and the mooncalves after their kind . . . Katie bent over her work even more attentively, concealing a very small smile.

Arthur pressed his hands tightly together, then trapped them between his knees. The curve of her white neck and cheek wrought intensely on his young feelings—the way her black hair lay sleek and yet lively on her small head, the familiarity with which the moon fingered every line in light and shadow. He drew a heavy breath and fixed his eyes on her hands, moving above the froth. She was humming now while she sewed, a lullaby rhythm, very simple, and he sat there helplessly, listening and watching, a child in the nursery of her unforeseen coziness.

He really did not know what to do, and he had stared too long. The moondrift of curtain began to bear a perilous resemblance to a bridal veil, and he felt a terrible impulse to do the unthinkable—to cast all discretion to the winds, fall on his knees, and propose marriage. He wondered what his parents would think of Katie. . . .

He knew very well what his parents would think of Katie. They would think that Katie was no better than she should be. Marriage was not to be thought of, but neither was it to be thought of that he would simply walk out of her room, leaving her alone, dazzling in moonlight on a moonlit bed.

He lurched to his feet again, stammering her name. She raised her eyes and impaled him on a green glance.

He could not know that she had just made up her mind for him to propose marriage and for her to accept. It was the lullaby that had done it, murmuring in her own ears its sweet domestic rhyme. She would marry Arthur, settle the matter once and for all. Mama, Clovelly, Octavia and Dawn would soon get used to the idea, and Katie, wedded, could then get along with her own life, thank you, as the Lord God and Noah intended her to do, with a mate at her side.

The chosen mate fell on his knees at the edge of the bed. It was not part of his agenda, and for one instant he was almost saved by the hardness of the floorboards and the chill that wove around his protruding ankles. "Katie," he said, before he could stop himself, "I love you." He reached up to embrace the cloud of curtain on her lap, determined to embrace her at the same time. He was not quite successful, she seemed to come and go like the moon, and to his utter dismay (with his parents gasping at his shoulder), he heard himself cry out, "Katie, will you marry me?"

"No," said Katie instantly. "But thank you just the same."

37

It was not at all what he had expected to hear. But then, in all fairness, it was not at all what she had expected to say. They looked at each other, him on his knees and her on her bed, and there quivered in the air between the two of them a most profound and undeniable sense of relief.

Arthur's father and mother stopped their gasping and went home. Katie's Mama and her three sisters faded into mist and moon. It was Katie's voice that broke the silence. "It's all right, Arthur," she said firmly. "You can go back to bed now."

"Katie—"

She shimmered before him. He knelt there, not knowing what he was, neither seducer nor suitor, divided. He was just beginning to understand that she was truly beautiful and that he wanted to fill his eyes with her, but she was telling him to go and he no longer knew whether he was very large or very small, very young or marvelously experienced. . . . "Katie!"

He might have stayed on his knees for the rest of the night, saying her name over and over, until the sun came through the window and took away the moon, but Mama's youngest daughter did, by sheer instinct, exactly the right thing. She leaned over, put her hands on his shoulders, and she gave him a kiss. It was a nice warming kiss, not quite sisterly but not quite ladylike either.

He staggered to his feet, found his way to the door, and put his hand on the knob. It occurred to him that perhaps he ought to bow, and he turned and did so. Solemnly, she bowed back.

Sighing faintly, he let himself out into the hallway, confused by a terrible happiness and a drowning sorrow.

"Hello, dear," said Clovelly, passing him.

There was no moonlight in the hall. Clovelly was a tall

branch of beauty, a shadow of blossom, a scent of something—lilac? summer? She reached out a long-fingered hand, touched him on the shoulder, and was gone.

"Hello, dear," said Arthur mistily, speaking to the empty corridor. Drunk on something quite inexpressible, he made his way back to his room, lay down on the bed, and fell into instant, though certainly not dreamless, sleep.

In her own room, Katie burrowed back into the pillow, tucked up in the moonlight. She thought briefly of Noah, and then of God, and she thought they must be the ones who had surprised her into saying no, just at the moment she had been arranging to say yes.

It was odd, but on the other hand it certainly augured well for her future that, at the age of seventeen, she had already rejected one husband. The very thought made her feel matronly, and she fell asleep almost at once, complacent and benign.

When, in the morning, she learned that Arthur Bean had left Falling Grove without waiting for his breakfast, she was not really sorry. Clovelly looked her over, drew almost the correct conclusions as to how the night had fared, and passed the report on to Mama, Octavia and Dawn, each of whom was deeply interested.

Only Mama said sentimentally, "Poor young man."

"He was looking very happy," Clovelly told her. "Later on, he'll feel sad, and then he'll be happy again. Poor Katie," she added, "she's the kind that's very good for men."

"Then I don't think she ought to marry," said Mama decidedly.

Clovelly said, "That's what I meant."

Five ∂

Communicating despair, Mama leaned her head on Cornelius's
shoulder. They were sitting close together on the sofa, and
he was holding her hand with a Darby-and-Joan fatuity
that could only be justified by half a century of married
life. Mama had always been able to supply this peculiar
reposefulness to the fathers of all her daughters, becoming
at times so roundly wifely that she seemed to blur at the
edges. This, combined with her gift for seeking advice
from gentlemen (they were delighted to give it, and she
felt no obligation to accept), made the days as pleasing as
the nights. When Cornelius came, even if he came only in
the line of business, he was always ridiculously happy.

At this moment, she had sought his advice, and he was
giving it freely. He patted the little hand that nestled in

his large one, and somehow it nestled even more as its owner said crisply, "Don't try to soothe me, Cornelius. I'm really very displeased." She then added, "Dawn, could you stop twittering, dear? I feel a headache coming on."

Dawn, lying on the floor near the window, her head on a cushion and her feet on the sill, said amiably, "You never get headaches, Mama." She then returned to her task which concerned an exact imitation of the love song of a goldcrown thrush on a whistle made of willow wood. Now, head delicately to one side, she judged the whistle's love song to be less expert than the bird's.

"It goes *down* on the last notes," Clovelly said, coming into the room with her arms full of decaying iron pipes.

"I know." Dawn licked the willow mouthpiece with a cat tongue, and put the whistle into her pocket. "Do you want one, Clovelly?"

"A thrush?"

"A whistle."

"Thank you," Clovelly said, "but I think not. They never do anything for me but cheep."

"You could imitate a sparrow." Dawn threw her head back, stared at the ceiling and yawned widely. Her pointed chin curved to the line of her throat, and the line of her throat curved to the thrust of her breasts, and Cornelius found himself thinking of nymphs, but respectfully as if he were in a museum.

"It's true I never get headaches," Mama said suddenly, "but I find it very difficult to think in a straight line."

Clovelly said, "Do you have to?" and dumped her iron pipes into the fireplace for storage until she could find some use for them. The chimney was full of squirrel nests, accumulated during the quiet years of the house's abandonment, and, the only time a boarder had tried to build a fire in it, thick rich smoke had poured through the room, rolling into the kitchen and up the stairwell. There had been, for weeks, a mysterious smell of burned mushrooms. "Where's Katie?" said Clovelly, thinking that her youngest sister might have a suggestion about what to do with the pipes. Katie was a bit of a jackdaw herself, but sometimes quite practical.

"Gone to town with Octavia. Dear Cornelius gave us some shopping money."

"Interest on your mortgage," dear Cornelius said rather wildly, not having as yet gotten it through his head that nobody here cared where money came from.

Mama said that was very clever of him, and then she sat and waited for someone to ask why she had announced that she was displeased. After a moment of silence, she put the question herself. "Why am I displeased? Because Katie refused Arthur Bean."

"I thought you were pleased," said Dawn, addressing the ceiling. "After all, she told us he wanted to *marry* her. You should be glad she said no."

"And rather enjoyed saying it, I gather," Clovelly remarked.

"Yes, but—" said Mama. "That was last week, and last week I thought it meant that she had given up all her foolish ideas about getting married. But now, when I asked her, she said no, just the idea of marrying Arthur."

"Dawn's fault," said Clovelly. "It's that business of Noah. The Lord God unfortunately made Dawn into a storyteller of infinite skill."

"In-fin-ite skill," Dawn agreed complacently. She sat up, pulled the whistle from her pocket and set it to her lips. This time, the goldcrown thrush dropped the last two notes in an absolutely perfect cadence. "See?" she said, and lay down again.

"If the Lord God believed in marriage," her mother said reasonably, "Adam and Eve would have been man and wife. I pointed that out to Katie—"

Clovelly interrupted. "—and Katie told you that Noah didn't get put out of the Garden of Eden, but Adam and Eve did, so it proved that Noah was the one who was doing the right thing."

"How did you know what she told me?"

"I'm afraid it's what *I* told *her*," Clovelly admitted. "I should have left the Bible to Dawn."

"No, no," Dawn said generously. "It's a very proper theological position. I'm proud of you."

"I think theology is beside the point," Mama said with dignity, and appealed to Cornelius. He nodded his head, having, by this time, no idea what they were talking about, and she went on, encouraged. "The point is, that it's all very well to be choosy about men, if you're not going to marry them, but Katie will end up by wrecking her life. Octavia thinks so, too." She took her hand away from Cornelius, folded it in her lap with the other one (white pigeons, so pretty) and sat very erect. "I'm sure Katie doesn't get her stubbornness from me."

Clovelly smiled down at Dawn. Dawn smiled up at Clovelly. The silence passing between them was discreet.

"Love and marriage," Mama said, "simply don't go together. Marriage pins you down, which is very unhealthy."

Cornelius shook his head, but with caution. He did not feel pinned down, and his health was excellent, but perhaps his experience was not the usual one. He had been lucky, and perhaps Katie would be lucky too. "She should marry," he said firmly, "if that's what she wants."

"She should be swept off her feet," said Clovelly aggravatingly.

43

"—and *then* married," Cornelius said.

Mama shot him a look of such fearful reproach that he reached for her hand rather anxiously. Naturally, she bestowed it on him, but her eyes said that he had betrayed her.

Dawn sat up and rested her forehead on her knees, curved like a sickle moon. "Katie *is* stubborn," she said in a thoughtful, muffled voice.

"It's her father coming out in her," Mama said. "I often wish that I could remember who he was. Dear man," she added fondly. "Of course, he never had any ties."

This footnote brought Cornelius to that brink of confusion which he so often arrived at when trying to follow Mama's mental processes. Clovelly, noting the cloud on his brow, undertook to explain. "Mama doesn't mean neckties, she means relatives."

Cornelius said "Ah," crossly, meaning that of course he knew what Mama meant, which was simply not true. He looked at his watch, said that he must be getting along, put down his love's hand, and got to his feet, feeling as ponderous as an elephant. Ponderously, he said, "If Katie wants to find a husband—and, mind you, I feel she is quite right . . ."

"Cornelius!" said his love.

He should have stopped there, but he lumbered on. "If Katie wants to find a husband, she ought to move away from here. No one's going to ask her to marry him if . . ." He stopped, absolutely appalled by what he had started to say.

". . . if he knows about us and our wicked ways," Clovelly finished for him.

Her voice sounded to Cornelius's ears like a small, very sharp dagger. Jeweled. He could feel himself shriveling inside.

"A very good point," Dawn agreed.

"But how clever of you, Cornelius!" Mama cried.

Shamed and despairing, he looked from one to the other to the third. They were all beaming at him. He blinked, and looked again, and it was still a fact. They were not angry at all, but sincerely pleased that he had put his finger so precisely on the very heart of Katie's problem. In another household, the dear ladies might rightfully have been cut to the quick, but then, in another household, Katie's determination to marry would not have seemed so odd. Basking in the sunshine of their approval, Mr. Porter felt suddenly graceful, not an elephant but a gazelle. He had been quite mistaken about the dagger in Clovelly's sweet voice.

"Of course," Mama was saying eagerly, "you're quite right. We must send Katie away." Promptly, she drooped. "But where would she go? And, oh, Cornelius—" a grace note of sorrow—"I shall miss her so!"

"But she'll live here after she's married, Mama," Dawn said, "and we'll all be in-laws."

"Whats?"

"In-laws, darling. They come with marriages."

Mama spread her hand across her eyes, then removed it and said bravely, "At least, it won't be Arthur Bean.— Cornelius, my love . . ."

Beautiful eyes, Cornelius thought distractedly.

"I shall leave it entirely to you," Mama said, got to her feet and moved into Cornelius's embrace. "It was all your idea in the first place, my dear. You are really *very* clever."

Clovelly was glowing at him, Dawn was glowing at him. He could not see anything of Mama except the top of her head, but he could feel her glowing against his chest. If Octavia were here, surely she would join them.

And Katie?

Well, Katie was a sensible young woman. All she really needed was to find a nice job in a nice household where a nice boy—Cornelius paused and amended his thinking. All Katie needed was to find worthy employment in a worthy household where a worthy young man . . .

He snapped his fingers. "I know the very place," he said. "Mrs. Cassidy and her son—*far* on the other side of town." His voice was the voice of a banker again, a gilt-edged stock. "The *very* place," he told them. "Leave it all to me."

They nodded, flowers in a meadow touched by his self-confident breeze. Leaving it to Mr. Porter was what they had planned to do all along, so that was what they did.

Six ⮌

The home of Mrs. Cassidy and her son Timothy Edward, into which Katie was to be so expertly inserted, was in a most respectable part of Falling Grove. Convenient to public transportation, shaded by stately elms, with a postbox at the corner and the Falling Grove Library scarcely two streets away, the house was large enough to be hard to maintain and small enough to annoy Mrs. Cassidy, who had been a Craddock by birth (the stiffnecked branch of that family) and who had married a Cassidy (the darlin' branch of *that* family). Before his early demise, Mr. Cassidy had imprudently gambled away his wife's fortune—extremely small, but it grew in her memory over the years—leaving only the house and the son.

Timothy, after being a very good small boy, moved on

47

to become a model adolescent, and he was now an upright and dutiful young man. At twelve, he had administered two paper routes and had never thrown a paper on anyone's lawn; at sixteen, he graduated to acting as messenger for the Superior Bank; at eighteen, he caught the eye of Cornelius Porter himself and was invited inside to count money. At twenty, as noted, he swam into his employer's mind and was selected to become a husband for Katie.

It was his own choice of the word *worthy* that had caused Cornelius to remember Timothy's existence. Impossible to find a young man more wholesomely worthy than Mrs. Cassidy's son. Marriage to Katie might, in fact, be just the thing needed to save him from the brink of total worthiness, and, at the same time (thought Cornelius Porter, whose relations with the Widow Thorne were certainly undermining his own more wholesome aspects) it would cause Timothy's god-awful mother to have a fit, which was a pleasing prospect.

The next morning, Cornelius called his young employee into his office and kept him standing. Timothy was a very square-shaped young man, even his trouser cuffs were square and his jaw most earnestly so. His hands and feet were rather large, which was nice, but the only true sign of Cassidy in him was his hair, which was faintly red and inclined to rumple.

Cornelius put his fingertips together like a bishop. "Your dear mother," he said without preamble, "is wearing herself out with housework." This was news to Timothy, who did most of the housework himself. His employer continued. "I respect her for it," he said, "but it's not right. What she needs is a nice maid—" He decided that a maid sounded dangerously frivolous, and made a correction. "A nice cleaning woman, to live in and to take the burden off her."

Timothy stared. His lips parted as though he were planning to do something besides breathe.

"I shall give you a raise," Cornelius said, speaking loudly, "and I have found the very girl for you." He did not actually state that the raise and the girl went together, but the financial nuance was implied and any intelligent member of the business community ought to be able to catch it.

Timothy not only caught it, he clung to it, banishing from his mind the memory of the last time there had been a maid in the Cassidy household. She had been a very nice maid, and a bonny one too, and perhaps it was the bonniness that had brought trouble with it—trouble from dawn to dusk and back again, tears on the girl's side and suffer-suffer-suffer on his mother's. He hesitated. "Mother doesn't like . . ." he began, and then, "Of course, I don't mean . . ." and then, desperately, "It's only that Mother may feel . . ."

"Katie," said Cornelius, may the Lord forgive him, "is very plain."

Timothy looked grateful. Cornelius, again reading him aright, added kindly, "I'll speak to your mother." His capitalist instinct told him that Mrs. Cassidy could easily be made to understand on which side her bread was buttered. If the butter eventually included a daughter-in-law—He skidded on his own metaphor, and waved a dismissing hand.

Timothy said thank you, thank you very much. "On behalf of my mother and myself," he explained earnestly, and added, "When can we expect Mrs. - er - Miss —?"

Cornelius started to say "Miss Thorne," then bethought himself that the members of the Cassidy household might have picked up rumors, although in their neighborhood it was unlikely they picked up anything. He said inventively, "MacPherson. Katie MacPherson. Her father was Scotch."

"Dead?" said Timothy.

"Decades ago," Cornelius said, then remembered that Katie had just turned seventeen. "She's an orphan," he announced, and heard himself adding, "Several times over." At this point, he testily told his employee that Miss Mac-Pherson would arrive on Thursday and to get back to work and not keep the depositors waiting.

Very confused but endlessly respectful, Timothy withdrew from the sanctum. As he closed the door behind him, his heart gave a slight skip. Although Katie MacPherson would probably turn out to be a skinny gray broomstick of a woman, or fat as a lard barrel, her coming would at least introduce something new—something unstructured and unpredictable—into that square, four-cornered house where Timothy lived his square, four-cornered life.

Katie arrived, duly, on Thursday evening, just as the clock in the tower of St. Morphrey's old church was chiming seven.

Her leavetaking had been exceptionally gala, with everyone present except Mr. Porter. His mark was upon the event, however, as he had instructed Katie to wear a very plain dress and to pin her hair on top of her head in a bun. She had added, by her own stroke of genius, a brown hat in which Clovelly normally kept clothespins.

There were a few boarders to see her off, including dear old Mr. Hermitage who acted as if he was giving the bride away, and a bouquet of dusty children. A yellow dog, the grocer's boy who had come to deliver a red cheese, and two mysterious hens who had followed him, were all lined up asymmetrically. Behind them bloomed Mama, Clovelly, Dawn and Octavia.

"It's just like a funeral," Katie told them appreciatively. Then she picked up her neat suitcase (which had belonged to the boarder that Dawn threw out of the house by moonlight—a sort of unearned dividend) and left them without further formalities, disappointing Mr. Hermitage who had prepared some very suitable thoughts for the occasion.

Now, as she stood upon the Cassidy doorstep, she remembered the farewell scene with satisfaction, and she presumed that her family would already be lamenting her absence, picturing a sort of artistic family-drooping, like lilies. As she raised her hand to knock, the resonance of St. Morphrey's faded, and a bird chirped.

The door opened before she could ask it to.

Katie saw a young man, sober in a gray suit, linear, his hair wet from having been plastered down, and she gave a faint involuntary nod. He was eminently suitable. He would fit the Ark.

"Miss MacPherson?" said Timothy, looking down at the top of a most peculiar brown hat.

Katie started to deny it, then remembered. "Yes—Katie MacPherson," she said and raised her green eyes to young Mr. Cassidy's.

The brown hat had not prepared him. For a moment, drowning in green seas, he thought there must have been a mistake, laid on his doorstep, and that, whoever this was, it could not be plain Katie MacPherson. But then she looked down demurely, and the view was all brown hat again, except for the hint of a curved chin. Anyone could have a curved chin, and Timothy knew he must have dreamed the eyes.

He said, "Come in, please," getting out of the doorway and (in spite of having dreamed the eyes) stumbling over his feet. "Mother's expecting you."

Katie, inspired, bobbed humbly. From what ancestral

deeps she had learned to do such a thing, Heaven only knew, but it bore witness to centuries of honest domestic service. Infinitely reassured, Timothy led her to his mother.

Mrs. Cassidy, with a keen eye for staging, had set herself up in a high-backed leather armchair, in the middle of the room. At first glance, Timothy's mother appeared to be a rather ordinary little woman, sweetfaced, like a pincushion. She had round eyes behind round glasses in a round face, graying ringlets arranged on her brow, and a generally round shape—all in sharp geometric contrast to her son. Her mouth was often ajar, because she was a great talker, but, when it was not, it was folded in martyrdom, and it was this combination that had caused Mr. Porter to select the word "god-awful." He did not mind the mouth ajar so much, but, when it folded, he despaired. It folded frequently—when she thought about her house, her neighbors, the state of the world, or her lifetime of sacrifices—and it folded most tightly when she thought about her husband, who had been unsatisfactory from the start.

She gazed now upon Katie, and what she saw was something dumpy in a dumpy brown hat and good stolid shoes. She had already told her neighbor, Mrs. Lukas, about the coming of Katie MacPherson into the Cassidy household. "The thoughtfulness of Mr. Porter," she had crooned, "I cannot tell you how touched I was," and then she had gone on to tell Mrs. Lukas how touched she was until the time came when Mrs. Lukas said she must get back to her lima beans, they were boiling over. (There were no lima beans.) Tomorrow, Mrs. Cassidy thought now as she gazed at Katie, tomorrow she would tell Mamie Lukas about the new girl's shoes. "One can always tell a good worker by her shoes," she would say. And the hat. Never had she seen a more reassuring hat.

Katie, after one swift glance around the room, gazed modestly at the floor. To her, Mrs. Cassidy was simply a future mother-in-law, and as such she seemed as acceptable as Noah's wife must have seemed to the wives of Shem, Ham and Japheth. Dawn, who had looked it up in the Old Testament, had said that all those wives were nameless, which was odd when one thought of all the begetting they had done. The Lord God who had written the Book had not been what you could call even-handed about the sexes.

At any rate, Mrs. Cassidy would do nicely.

"Well," said Mrs. Cassidy, unwittingly returning the compliment, "all very satisfactory, I'm sure. Mr. Porter recommends you, Katie. I'm sure you must feel very grateful to Mr. Porter."

The brown hat bobbed. It would have been more elegant if Mrs. Cassidy had addressed her as Miss MacPherson, but the matter was trivial. Soon they would be related to each other, mother-in-law and daughter-in-law in proper kinship.

"Your room is on the third floor," Mrs. Cassidy said. "My son will take you up." She folded her lips a trifle and touched the stick that lay against the chair arm. "I cannot climb stairs very well," she said. "My knee hampers me." After a moment, she added bravely, "It's nothing."

Timothy, who had lived with that hampering knee for a long time, sighed and picked up Katie's suitcase. "If you'll follow me, Miss MacPherson . . ."

"Yes, sir," said Miss MacPherson very promptly, then gave her intended mother-in-law a pleasant nod and followed her intended husband out. As she went through the door into the hallway, her skirt gave a slight twitch, but, luckily, Mrs. Cassidy was somewhat myopic and, for the moment, nothing marred her conviction that Mr. Porter was a prince among men.

"It's three flights," said Timothy, apologizing.

"I don't mind." The stairs were steep and the way long to the maid's room under the sloping roof, but Katie followed him, light as a sparrow in her respectable shoes and peering out interestedly from under the brim of her brown hat. She liked the house, she liked the location, and she liked Timothy.

He stopped suddenly on the top landing and pushed open the door. Aglow with satisfaction, Katie smiled up at him, but he was already across the room and had thrown open its one narrow window. He mopped his brow; the room was hot.

Katie looked about her. A slanty ceiling and a slanty floor. A rocking chair with long rockers, a glum bureau with a bulging front and one drawer missing like a gap tooth. A bed with a mattress that sagged where it did not lump. No matter, she would soon be sharing a better bed. "Where's the bathroom?" she said forthrightly.

Timothy turned crimson. "There's only one. It's on the s-second floor. It—you—"

"That's fine," said Katie. In the Thorne house, there was also only one bathroom, and since everyone shared it—the family and the boarders and the children, and sometimes Mr. Porter—the hallway outside had become a kind of plaza where friends met and talked. She remembered only one objector, a small boy who had come to visit on a hot afternoon with no one's permission and who had howled with rage when told to wait in line. He had taken instant revenge, been told calmly to do his own mopping-up, and by evening was as democratic a little monster as one could ask for. Three to a bathroom, in Katie's view, was privacy indeed.

How quiet she is, Timothy thought, as the tide of embar-

54

rassment ran down inside his collar and cooled. A mouse, really. Mother would like having a mouse around. "Is everything all right?"

"It's lovely," said Katie and pulled off her hat.

He saw the top of her head, neat and small, with a great bun of black hair skewered tight on top of it. His eyes traveled down, itemizing as if she were a bank statement: neckline, high and prim; skirt, long enough to be decent; shoes, twin models of decorum. If the curve from neck to waist was rather rounded, if the skirt swayed a little at the hips because Katie swayed a little, if the respectable shoes covered feet that were very tiny—well, Timothy had been brought up never to linger over his thoughts.

"Thank you," said Katie, smiled the smile he had missed earlier, and once more raised her eyes to his.

He had not dreamed them. They were as green as he remembered—moss green, grass green, emerald green, green at the bottom of a well, green at the heart of a wave, hallucinating green.

She's just a nice little cleaning woman, said half of Timothy's mind. *You're drowning,* said the other half, *what a glorious way to drown.*

Katie said, "I think your mother is calling you, Mr. Cassidy." The white lids with their feathery fringe of soft lashes came down over the green eyes.

Timothy gulped, cried out, "Yes, mother, I'm coming," and fled the scene, nearly knocking his only parent flat on the second landing. She had come clumping up the stairs to find out whether Timothy was taking too long, and why, but she forgave him, merely murmuring something about her bad knee. "I was anxious," she explained. "You took so long."

He told his first lie. He said, "The window stuck."

55

She patted the strong right arm that had manfully pushed that window up, then leaned on it heavily and resumed her limp. "I must say," she said, "that she seems to be a nice little woman. Quite satisfactory." She waited for him to answer, and, when he did not, she said, "Timothy? Don't you think she's satisfactory?"

"Yes," said Timothy, "I do." He spoke loudly in order to be heard above the pounding of his heart.

Seven ❧

Katie estimated that Timothy could be brought to the point of proposing within the week. Shortly thereafter, they would be married.

Scheduled so briskly, she was able to bear with Mrs. Cassidy, who was not easy to bear with and who appeared to look upon Katie as a new broom that could be sent into all the neglected corners. Katie obliged her. The silver tea set, Craddock not Cassidy, gleamed as never before. The banisters were polished, the floor shone, even the fireplace was robbed of winter ashes. Mrs. Cassidy was frankly astonished, since, added to all this lustre, was gravy without lumps, lamb without garlic. The latter astonished her especially; it had been Mrs. Cassidy's understanding that the lower classes were partial to garlic.

By the third day, Mrs. Cassidy was referring to Katie as a nice little body. She said as much to her son, at the supper table. "Quite a nice little body. With a bit of training, I shall find her very acceptable."

Timothy swam up out of his dish of caramel custard. The recipe was Octavia's, and it was as smooth as thick cream, parting lusciously to the seeking spoon. On top of it were tiny globules of golden sugar. "Yes," said Timothy, responding to his mother, "she is."

"Is *what?*" his mother said.

"A nice little b—" He choked on custard, the uncompleted phrase causing his mind to ripple slightly. Some day, he would take that nice little body into his arms, hold it against his heart, and it would be so soft, so soft. He would ask her to marry him, she would say yes, and his whole world—which had never, somehow, been quite right—would suddenly all fall into place. He sighed very deeply.

"I believe you're getting a cold," his mother said sharply. His father had persisted in getting colds, which he mastered with whiskey. His wake had been intemperately merry.

"No," said Timothy, "I am not." It was not often that he contradicted his mother, and he felt heartened by the small exercise. Then Katie came in from the kitchen, and he was further heartened, although an enveloping apron was tied around her ring-span waist and her hair was skewered into that intimidating bun. . . .

Once, he had seen Katie with her hair down. He had come running up the stairs one morning to that third-floor bedroom, with some message from his mother about andirons, and he had seen her, gazing at herself in the little mirror above the bureau, humming like a drowsy bee, her back to the door and her hair hanging down to her waist. Clouds of it, black as thunder and full of lights. Mermaid's hair, Timothy had thought, standing there on the landing and swaying foolishly. Never mind the established fact that all mermaids have golden hair. No golden-haired mermaid would be half so beautiful. *Beautiful* meant *Katie.* He wanted to take a long step into her room and to bury his face in those black-glinting clouds.

Her hair would be scented, he thought—light like lemon, or rich like cinnabar. But he did not know what cinnabar smelled like, he did not even know what cinnabar was—a spice, a gem, a tree? It had come upon him with terrible force that he was only a bank clerk and that he would never know how to tell a young girl how beautiful she was. After a moment, he had turned away quietly and gone down the stairs. No knowing what happened to the andirons.

Now, when Katie set a cup of coffee at his elbow, he lifted his eyes from his spoon. "Thank you," he said.

"You're welcome, sir." When she wanted to, Katie could make her voice pure velvet, a useful talent inherited from her mother. A besotted boarder had once told Mama that he could rock himself to sleep in the velvet of that voice, and Mama had told him (velvetly) that it was a beautiful thing to say, but later on, privately and with a squeak of glee, she had passed the thought on to her daughters. Disloyal, perhaps, but in the long run the boarder would certainly have preferred to be laughed at than forgotten.

"Ma'am," said Katie, putting the other cup of coffee down alongside Mrs. Cassidy's well-polished custard dish. (Like the cat licked it, Katie thought complacently.) "Will there be anything more?"

59

"Not at the moment," Mrs. Cassidy said, rather grandly. "Timothy, my dear, something more for you?"

"No, Mother. Thank you." Forever and forever, Mother would be there, Timothy-my-dearing him, across the breakfast table, the supper table, across the hall, the living room, the porch. He would spend his days, forever and forever, behind a bank wicket, and he would spend his nights, forever and forever, in a narrow bed. His mother often told him that she did not know how she would ever live without him, he was all that she had. She made it clear that her knee was bad, that her health was delicate, and that she was easily upset by emotional situations because she was sensitive. She was—beginning and end of it—his mother, and he knew his duty.

He looked up at Katie. Katie looked down at him with her green eyes, then she smiled and left the room.

Half an hour later, he announced to his mother that he felt the need of a breath of fresh air and would take a turn around the block. She granted permission and failed to notice that he left by the back door. To reach the back door, one went through the kitchen.

Katie was there, bending over the sink, stirring soapy water about with a long-handled spoon and muttering what appeared to be an incantation. Actually, the drain had stopped itself up while she was washing pots and pans (she was a somewhat chaotic cook) and she was longing now for Clovelly, who had a real gift for drains.

Timothy stood silent in the doorway and watched her. The back of Katie's neck was alabaster-white. Unlike cinnabar, he knew what alabaster was, and his thumb ached with longing to trace that perfect line, as a sculptor's thumb might follow the curve of Aphrodite's neck. He knew about Aphrodite, too, from reading Greek legends in grade school, but he did not know why his thumb ached, which shows the limitations of public education.

After a while, he breathed deeply and said, "Can I help you, Katie?"

She glanced back at him over her shoulder, shook her soapy wrists, and smiled. It was the Noah's Ark smile, the baited trap, and it was perfectly fair to use it because she intended to be a model wife. "Oh, thank you, sir," said demure little Katie, laying it on a bit too thick.

Timothy was struck to his diffident heart. "Don't call me *sir,* please, Katie."

"Mr. Timothy, then," said Katie dewily.

"Timothy," Timothy said.

"Oh," said Katie, then, very softly, "Timothy."

He felt suddenly so strong that he crossed the kitchen floor in two long strides and took the spoon out of her hand. "Something's stuck in the drain," he said. "It happens all the time. The drainpipe's too narrow." He reached under the sink for a long piece of wire kept for this precise emergency and stabbed it through the drain hole. There was a faint gurgle, as of dying fishbones, and a sudden rush of water going down.

"How clever of you!" Perfectly sincere this time, Katie clasped her hands, found them very wet and rubbed them down along her skirt. He looked at her, and she bit her lip and said, oh dear, she must be a fright. "I didn't expect you," she said, "but I'm glad you came."

"You're not a fright," said Timothy, very gravely. "You're beautiful."

"Oh, no," said Katie, "I'm not beautiful at all." The corners of her mouth tucked in, while she waited for him to deny this.

"Yes, you are beautiful. You're very beautiful." The

rhythm struck him as almost poetic, and poetry, as usual, encouraged rashness. "But you're even more beautiful with your hair down your back," he said daringly.

She gasped, very nicely. "Oh, Mr. Timothy, when did you ever—?" That would be the time, she thought calmly, when he had come up the stairs and stood there staring at her in her own mirror, a frame for her, very becoming.

"You were in your room," he told her. "I came to tell you about the andirons. . . ." (What andirons? Katie wondered, but far be it from her to interrupt.) "Your hair was down your back, and you looked like a mermaid. I know I shouldn't have stood there looking at you when you didn't know that I was looking."

"I wouldn't have minded," Katie said shyly.

He took a step toward her, then stopped. "I mustn't . . ."

But he must. Katie took a step toward him, and somehow managed to make it look like a retreat. She breathed his name.

"Katie," he said, and swept her into his arms. Or he thought he did. Anyway, she was suddenly there.

The top of her head came just under his chin. Less romantically, one ill-placed hairpin in its skewered bun scratched him sharply. He unclasped his hands from her waist and raised them to her hair. It took only a second to undo Katie MacPherson's respectable coiffure and to bring the mermaid's tresses streaming down. Timothy buried his face in cloud and scent, and he groaned.

She stood there in his arms, nestling and stroking him to stop his trembling. Oh, poor young man, she thought, it's all new to him. "There," she murmured, "there, there now," the way Dawn would murmur to a puppy or a young bird.

62

"Oh, Katie," he said deeply. What he wanted to do was to lift her, her round arms around his neck and his strong arms under her knees, and to carry her upstairs to that small room on the third floor. And then—oh, then! the suppressed Cassidy within him shouted—then, he would know exactly how to proceed.

"Katie!" Timothy cried. "Katie, will you marry me?"

"Yes," said Katie with real enthusiasm.

Eight ∿

It took Timothy two days to gather up enough strength to tell his mother.

Katie had offered to do it herself, but Timothy hastily said no and kissed her tenderly on the brow. He longed to behave in an even more positive manner, but the Craddock in him had always been permitted ascendancy over the Cassidy, and, after that first delirious embrace from which he still tingled, he had forsworn excess. This was quite satisfactory to Katie, who had not tingled, and she agreed to wait, at the same time setting a private deadline in her own mind. Timothy, looking long and deep into those eyes, thought her patience was adorable.

On Sunday, after church, he brought himself to the

pitch. He had sat with his mother in St. Morphrey's front pew, thinking secularly about Katie, while his mother, devoutly, was thinking about salvation and laying her plans to be among the Elect. Timothy would also be there, of course, and certainly Mr. Cornelius Porter, but her late husband would not.

Occupied with these spiritual arrangements, she scarcely heard the Reverend Beasley's sermon, which was full of *whereas* and *insomuch* and studded with audible semicolons, all quite easy to ignore. St. Morphrey's congregation was small, restless and dull of mind, and, the longer the sermon, the more it shuffled its feet and cleared its throat and thought small, restless and dull thoughts. Perversely, at the moment of escape, it always lingered, each member suddenly eager to assure the minister that it had been a fine sermon and explain why they had not been in church last Sunday and would not be there next. The Reverend Beasley nodded his courteous nod, smiled his faded smile, and thought about his noon meal. The potatoes would be watery, the meat stringy, the beans limp; it was something to rely on in a world that was fugitive and passing and a hereafter that was not immediately available.

"A fine sermon," Mrs. Cassidy advised him, presenting her Sunday smile at the church porch. "I feel quite uplifted."

He pressed her hand. He did not much like Mrs. Cassidy, which was unchristian of him, but he rather liked Timothy. One never need say anything to the young man, because he never said anything to one. Mr. Beasley's Heaven was certainly going to be a place where no one expected him to exhort, to sermonize, or to be an inspiration. He said, "Thank you so much," although perhaps the hand-pressing would have been sufficient.

65

Mrs. Cassidy, still wishing to discuss her uplift, gave way reluctantly to the stout man behind her, who, she happened to know, only came to church for business reasons. She said as much to Timothy, as she put her hand possessively through his arm.

He said yes, or possibly no. They crossed the street in silence and went down the block, Mrs. Cassidy savoring Judgment Day and Timothy turning over in his mind how best to break his unlikely news.

"I told Katie to serve browned potatoes with the roast pork," his mother remarked, the name of the beloved very prosaic on her tongue. "I hope she remembers."

"Katie always remembers," Timothy said, and then he drew a long brave breath. On the crest of it, he said, "Mother, you like Katie, don't you?"

"Yes, indeed." Her voice was amiable, meaning that there is nothing like the assurance of a good Sunday roast, served by a good biddable girl. Training, she thought, is all, and she wondered if the Reverend had had something of the sort in mind this morning when he spoke of being obedient in all things. She must ask him the source of the quotation—it was very apt.

Upon this, feeling both intellectual and Christian (a heady combination), she beamed upon her son. "I might go so far as to say," she went so far as to say, "that I find her most capable. Most capable." A good choice of words; she rested on it.

"I'm going to marry her," said Timothy.

"She certainly is," his mother assured him, fully occupied with her own mental processes.

"Mother! You're not listening to me." He was used to not being listened to, but, unless he told her now, he would never be able to tell her. A green-eyed girl streaked across his vision, and he raised his voice. "Mother, I am going to marry Katie MacPherson."

His mother stopped dead in her tracks and made a curious sound, not unlike a gargle. She then sagged on Timothy's arm. Timothy stiffened and stared straight ahead, something he had never done before when she sagged on his arm. She promptly stopped sagging, became rigid, and cried "Timothy!" managing to get a good deal into the three syllables—shock, grief, and lonely widowhood.

Timothy swallowed hard. "Yes, Mother?" His jaw stayed firm, but the rest of him was losing confidence.

"You cannot," said Mrs. Cassidy, "be serious."

"I am serious," said Timothy, praying for the strength to prove it. His mother's mouth was opening and closing most unbecomingly. In another moment, she would be telling him that he was all she had in the world, that his father had wrecked her life, and that her leg was bad. In another moment, she would totter.

Dear Lord! he prayed inwardly, although it was unfair to call on his Maker after ignoring Him in church all morning. Grasping for straws, he clutched a cliché. "You won't be losing a son, Mother," he said. "You'll be gaining a daughter."

It was not a useful comment. The last thing on earth that Mrs. Cassidy wished to gain was a daughter, and she had no intention of doing so. Poised on the brink of tottering, she cast a glance upward and encountered her son's jaw. It was jutting. He had not jutted his jaw at her since he was eleven years old; at eleven, he had been briefly difficult, and he was being difficult now. She must make short work of the matter. "I never heard such nonsense," she said firmly.

67

Timothy shook his head. "We'll talk about it when we get home." His hand on her elbow was urgent, and she mistook his anxiety for mutiny. "I feel faint," she said, even more firmly.

"All the better reason to get home," he told her, and he gave up praying to the Lord and simply prayed that Katie would be on the doorstep. Katie would know what to do.

Katie, of course, was on the doorstep, and Katie, of course, knew what to do. One quick look at Mrs. Cassidy's face told her that Timothy had broken the glad news. She cast upon her beloved the most ravishing smile in her inventory, which could hardly fail to stiffen his backbone, and then, cooing like a dovecote, she flew to his mother and proceeded to overwhelm her with kindness. There was more than a little of Mama in Katie, and she could, when called upon, be more cloying and honey-sweet than a rose petal.

"There, there," she murmured now, and she shoved Mrs. Cassidy into the front room while appearing to guide her tottering footsteps and to comfort her outraged soul. The speed of attack gave the good lady no time for action and no breath for speech. She found herself dumped tenderly into the armchair, while Katie knelt at her feet and undid her shoes.

"Timothy," said Katie, "get your mother a glass of water."

"Yes," said Timothy. "Katie, I told her about—about us."

"Yes, dear," said Katie kindly. "I see you did."

Mrs. Cassidy found her voice and was about to make use of it in a shriek, when Katie, who was now enjoying herself a good deal, said, "I shall call you Mother Cassidy."

The vocal chords of Mother Cassidy tied themselves into a knot. Their owner croaked and turned mauve. Timothy, who had brought the glass of water and was standing around helplessly, turned a pale shade of oyster. Then, "You are *not* going to marry my son," his mother said, with awful distinctness.

"Just a little sip, dear," said Katie, wilfully compassionate.

"You are not going to—" The glass at her lips interfered with speech, and she raised an angry hand to strike it away.

"There!" said Katie and deftly inserted the little sip, spilling not a drop. "Mr. Porter is going to be *so* pleased." She touched her victim's lips with a nice clean handkerchief, and then added blandly, "So pleased that Timothy and me are going to get married, that is."

Mrs. Cassidy's angry hand paused in midair. There was a very long silence, a spreading silence. After it had carpeted the entire room, Mrs. Cassidy found her voice. "Mr. Porter?" she said. "Mr. *Porter?*"

"It was," said Katie simply, "his secret hope."

The room fell silent once more, and wheels began to spin slowly inside Mrs. Cassidy's head. Timothy's observation about not losing a son but gaining a daughter acquired sudden merit. There was no doubt much good in this MacPherson girl, she was certainly an able housekeeper, Cornelius Porter was a man of exceptionally sound judgment. . . . The wheels ceased their slow spinning and began to hurtle. A mother's love can encompass any sacrifice; only fools fail to recognize which side their bread is buttered on. . . .

An additional thought, of unpaid help in perpetuity, also flickered across Mrs. Cassidy's mind, but she dis-

69

missed it as unworthy. She would accept this child for her own sweet sake.

She raised her head. "Life must go on," she said. The statement was received calmly. "I suppose I must take the back seat now," she said. This, too, being received calmly, she then announced that she was exhausted. "I am exhausted," she said.

Timothy leaped to take one arm. Katie took the other. In the merest trice, Mrs. Cassidy found herself lying on her own bed, two soft pillows to support her, a fringed blanket to keep her cozy, the curtains drawn to cradle her collapse. They were already leaving her alone. They were tiptoeing out of the room, saying hush, hush, hush.

Timothy closed the door behind them and drew Katie into his arms. "Oh, you *are* wonderful," he said, holding her tight. "Katie, Katie! You said just the right thing about Mr. Porter wanting us to marry." He had not supposed that he was the kind of man who would exult over his fiancée's outrageous fictions, but there it was. He was that kind of man.

"It happened to be true," said Katie, with satisfaction. It was not often that facts coincided so nicely with necessity.

Timothy, who knew it could not be true, suppressed an inner cockcrow. He had fallen so far from grace that now he was content to believe her, even when he knew she lied. Used to dealing with bank balances, deficits, surpluses and accounts receivable, all of which can be interpreted to mean practically anything, he was not really that far out of his depth. *"Mrs. Cassidy,"* he said, in reverent italics.

Katie said, "What about her?"

"Katie Cassidy," he explained, and then laughed triumphantly. "You, Katie darling, *you.*"

The sound of it startled her a little. Katie Cassidy she would become, not Katie Thorne. Would Mama mind? Would Clovelly? Dawn? Octavia? She must let them know as soon as possible, it was only proper. She leaned backwards to look up into Timothy's face. "I'm going to have a—a nuptial party," she said. "Unless that's what you have *after* you're married. Anyway, I want you to meet all my family."

"Family? I thought you were an orphan."

She stared at him. "What ever made you think that?"

"Mr. Porter said so."

"You must have heard it wrong. Mr. Porter couldn't possibly have forgotten about Mama."

Timothy thought for a moment and was able to accept a mother-in-law, though it came as a surprise.

"And my three sisters," said Katie.

"Three?" He thought for another moment, slightly longer, and was able to accept three sisters-in-law.

"Clovelly and Dawn and Octavia."

They rang in his ears like bells, and he smiled with quick pleasure. Then his voice deepened, and he said, "Your father is dead?"

"I don't really—" Katie hesitated, having been about to say that she had no idea whether her forever-unidentified father was above ground or below it. Indeed, just for an instant—may the Lord forgive her—she was dreadfully tempted to say that Mr. Porter was her father (Mr. Porter would have been *so* pleased), but she conquered the impulse, sensing that it would only create muddle. "Yes, my father's dead," she said gravely, trusting that, if he happened to be alive, he was not sensitive about such matters.

Timothy said he was sorry to hear it. He said he would look forward to meeting his future mother-in-law and his three future sisters-in-law, and then he said, "Oh, my darling," and reached for his future wife.

She flowed into his arms, fitted herself just under his chin, and said into his collar, "I'll tell them to come on Tuesday."

"That's too soon." He gazed down at the raven hair and pondered that, now, it belonged to him. "Mother won't like such short notice."

"But Mama will like it," Katie told him, "and so will Clovelly and Dawn and Octavia."

The second time round, the chime of their names was easier to resist. "But, my darling . . ."

"Tuesday," said Katie.

He felt the smallest twinge of dismay. It was disloyal of him, and he was able to shake it off at once so that all he actually said was "Oh."

She lifted her head. He lowered his. Her mouth was like velvet, like honey. Never again, he thought helplessly, would anything taste so sweet. Somehow, he had not expected . . . No one had ever told him . . . He had never dreamed . . .

Tuesday could take care of itself.

Nine ⁓

The Thornes descended. There is no other word for it.

The moment that Katie, waiting on the Cassidy front steps, saw them descending, from the reckless aristocracy of the hired car on which Mr. Porter had insisted, she realized how much she had missed them.

She flew down the steps and into the arms of all four of them at once. To Timothy, waiting in the doorway and strangling with his anxiety, they sounded like a beehive and they looked like butterflies. Each was more beautiful than the last, and lo, his Katie was the most beautiful of all.

He sprang down the steps, feeling unaccountably like a Greek god (that ought to have warned him), and the tallest of the sisters, the one with the swan throat and the dark brows, said huskily, "Oh, you must be Timothy!" and pulled him into the circle. He was smothered instantly by Mama, who stood on tiptoe as he bent to her embrace and put her arms around his neck. He straightened, and she came up with him.

It was thus that his own mother saw him—flushed and young and Greek and wearing Mama like a necklace. The news that she was about to acquire so many relatives had not sat too well on Mrs. Cassidy; moderation in all things, and they would expect to be fed. She had carefully instructed Katie to provide nothing stronger than tea and sugar biscuits, but the sense of excess persisted and now here was Timothy, surrounded by a womanhood which was aggressively non-Craddock.

However, she knew her duty and she did it, a handshake to the one who must be the parent and a bow to each sister. By the time she came to Dawn, Mrs. Cassidy had developed a real sense of foreboding. The four of them, coming all at once, were a hothouse of blooms, a zoo of talk, a jungle (she feared) of emotions. She continued to remind herself that she knew her duty, and she clung to the thought of Mr. Porter, who was going to be *so* pleased.

Mama, about to sail through the front door ahead of everybody, suddenly turned back and ripped her white glove from her white hand. She had worried a trifle about her gloves, because her daughters flatly refused to wear any, but dim in Mama's memory was a pair of long gloves at midnight and a young man in uniform who had removed them gently from her undeniably charming hands and dropped a kiss into each soft palm. She could not now recall his name, but it might well have been Alexander, and she had never been able to maneuver any other young man, in uniform or out of it, to precisely that refined gesture.

It had not, however, been the memory of Alexander (Frederick? Lionel?) that turned her back in the doorway. It was the feeling that she ought to have taken her glove off *before* she shook hands with Katie's mother-in-law, and, no matter how much she disapproved of the whole idea of in-laws, Mama did want to do things right. Accordingly, she shook hands all over again, and murmured her way into the front room, saying how-lovely to the Boston fern, how-distinguished to the walnut breakfront, and how-elegant to the large rug of many colors which was not quite an Oriental.

Once they were all seated, Katie said she would fetch the tea tray. Timothy placed a footstool for his mother. Mama rolled her white gloves into a snowball and detained her youngest child. "Love," she said, "what *have* you done to your hair?"

"Put it up," said Katie, "sort of." She had made an honest effort to compromise between the bun recommended by Mr. Porter, who was responsible for her success, and the down-the-back recommended by Timothy. The result was neither prim nor abandoned, but more like an unfinished nest.

"It's quite terrible, darling," Mama said, with her usual candor. "Do let it down."

Katie shrugged and removed the four hairpins which were falling out anyway. The heavy dark mass tumbled around her shoulders and streamed down her back. Mrs. Cassidy gasped. Mrs. Cassidy was not a student of beauty, but there was no question whatever of the effect of that waterfall of black hair on her respectable ex-cleaning woman. Katie MacPherson stood there, in the middle of the Cassidys' front room, looking as immoral as a wood nymph.

Katie tossed the culprit strands back from her face and

began to braid them, not in response to Mrs. Cassidy's gasp but because they would certainly tangle with the tea tray. Her fingers shuttled quickly, and in a moment she had tossed the long thick rope over her shoulder and was almost respectable again.

The harm, however, had been done. Katie with her hair down her back had put Mrs. Cassidy's mind onto something she had forgotten. Something she had heard from a neighbor, a Mrs. Bottle who had heard it from another neighbor who had since moved away. Something about a house at the other end of Falling Grove, where a widow lived. A widow with two—or was it three? or was it four?—daughters. An impropriety?

An affront to decent people.

Mrs. Cassidy forced herself to settle back in her armchair. She must, of course, proceed very carefully, since Katie had been sent by Mr. Porter himself and Mr. Porter himself was a man of sound judgment, being a banker. Still, he was a man before he was a banker, and all men were easy marks. One had only to remember Mr. Cassidy, who had not only been an easy mark but who had been absolutely delighted about it. She put her hands into her lap and held them there.

"Can I help you, Katie?" Timothy said. "In the kitchen?" Katie smiled and nodded, and he followed her out of the room, all but stumbling over his eager feet.

She is no good, Mrs. Cassidy thought, her fingers knitting themselves together. *She is a wanton and she is no good, even if her name is MacPherson.* The name checked her. The name of that family, at the far edge of town and with all those daughters and That Reputation, was certainly not MacPherson. It was . . . It was . . .

She leaned forward suddenly and tapped the knee (so

76

rounded under the rounded skirt) of Katie's mother. "Mrs. MacPherson," she said, "it is such a pleasure to have you with us."

"Why, thank you." Mama was only momentarily confused by the unfamiliar name, remembering swiftly that her darling Cornelius had chosen it for her darling Katie. "But it's Katie that's the MacPherson," she added pleasantly. "I'm a Thorne. That is, my late husband was a Thorne."

"Thorne!" The named clicked triumphantly into the slot that Mrs. Cassidy's mind had prepared for it.

"That is," Mama went on, incautiously chatty, "my last late husband was a Thorne. My first husband was the MacPherson."

"I thought," said Mrs. Cassidy, closing in with icy calm, "that Katie was your *youngest* daughter."

"So she is," Mama agreed brightly. There was a faint stirring of the air in the room, a summer-balm breeze, as Clovelly, Octavia and Dawn turned their heads delicately on their delicate necks to gaze dreamily at their maternal parent. Their expressions were akin to that of some enthralled scientist watching a totally unpredictable and wonderful bug.

Mama, sensing something dimly awry, was unable to put her finger on it in any logical fashion. She believed in logic, but only the way one might in angels—too remote to be helpful. She was about to offer some disarming comment about not being good at dates, but she was not given time.

"Then Katie is not a MacPherson," said Mrs. Cassidy, speaking from Olympus. "She is a *Thorne*."

"Well, yes," Mama agreed, then got in her line about not being good at dates, and gave that helpless little laugh at which she excelled. It had been known to reduce strong men to putty; there were days when it hummed through Cornelius Porter, even at his desk, like a madrigal.

It did not hum through Mrs. Cassidy. She removed her hands from her lap, spread them flat on the arms of her chair, and raised herself up. Small though she was, she was about to tower.

At this moment, Katie came back into the room, the sugar biscuits and the tea on the best tray, Timothy behind her with his hands full of spoons.

"Timothy," said his mother, speaking loud and clear, "she is not a MacPherson. She is a Thorne."

Timothy stared. The information conveyed nothing to him.

Katie put the tray down on the center table, and then turned to Mrs. Cassidy. "Well, I might have been a Mac-Pherson," she said calmly. "I don't *know* that I'm not."

Mama said, with real pleasure, "But that's quite true, Katie! You might easily have been a MacPherson. It sounds very distinguished, and I'm sure your father was a very distinguished man." She gazed up at the ceiling, struggling for memory. "If I could only remember his name . . . MacPherson, MacPherson. No, I don't think that was it."

It was Mrs. Cassidy's moment. She achieved her aim of towering. She extended her right arm dramatically, and she pointed her index finger straight at Katie. "You are a whore," said Mrs. Cassidy. Unfamiliarity with the word, which she had never gone so far as to speak before, caused her to mispronounce it. Both the W and the H were balefully audible.

Dawn said pedantically, "I believe the W is silent," and turned to Clovelly for confirmation. Clovelly nodded and said that the W was indeed silent, as in *who* but not as in *why*. They agreed with each other, gently, that the English language was peculiar.

Katie failed to benefit from the exchange. "I am *not* a whore!" she said indignantly, coming out very strong on the W.

"You are!" said Mrs. Cassidy, and she reached for the chair behind her for support.

Timothy, with the training of many years, leaped to her side and saw, too late, how this divided the room— Thornes on one side, Cassidys on the other. "Mother!" he said hoarsely. "Mother, I'm sure you don't mean . . ."

His hands were full of spoons, and she was able to push him away quite easily. "Timothy," she said sternly, "that wicked girl has lied to you from the start. She is not a MacPherson, and she never was. She is one of those dreadful Thornes from the other side of town, and her mother does not even know the name of the man—the man who . . ." One could hear her voice reeling. "Everybody knows what these women are, everybody knows about that house. Timothy!" She clutched him back.

Even Timothy had heard about *that* house, although certainly very little. It was unthinkable that Katie—*his* Katie . . . He cast a quick look at her and felt as if he had burned his fingers. She was a blaze of green fire.

"Timothy Cassidy," said Katie, sparks flying from every consonant, "tell your mother that I am not a whore."

He hesitated. It was the bank teller in him, checking every column to be sure it added up right. If Katie belonged to *that* family—And how could he tell? How could he be sure? Something very like a sob welled up inside him, and he choked it down, feeling as lost as a five-year-old. He said, stuttering, "B-but, Katie—Katie, of course I don't—I don't b-b-believe . . ."

The hesitation was fatal.

79

Katie drew herself up, an avenging angel, a tempest, a long-clawed tiger kitten. Her green eyes struck clean through him. "Maybe I am a Thorne," said Katie, "and maybe I am not. Maybe I am a MacPherson, and maybe I am not. But I know one thing," she finished with terrible scorn, "I am never going to be a Cassidy. Not—" She spit it out. "—not if you were the last man on earth." She spun on her heel, her thick dark hair flying behind her like the mane of some fierce, intractable unicorn, and she ran out of the house.

Across Mrs. Cassidy's face, there spread a smile of total satisfaction. Slowly, regally, she let herself sink into her chair. "A little pot," Mrs. Cassidy announced to the room at large, "is soon hot."

Mama rose. *"Honi soit qui mal y pense,"* she said, very musically. The phrase had come to her unbidden, from that long-ago and sweet memory of the young man who had stripped the white gloves from her hands. She recollected now: he had been French, and his name had not been Alexander, or Frederick, or Lionel. His name had been Peter, pronounced Pierre.

On this note of triumph, she floated quite beautifully out of the room.

Mrs. Cassidy, who had no French, believed she had been the object of an ancient curse, and she shrank back a little. Clovelly, seeing this, rather meanly stepped forward, swept her an exquisite curtsey, almost to the floor, smiled up at mother and son, and then made her own exit.

Dawn took her place. She lifted Mrs. Cassidy's two hands between her own and held them briefly. "You should pronounce it *hore*, Mrs. Cassidy," she murmured. "Not *whore*." She said the last word with a light puff, like someone blowing out a tiny candle.

Mrs. Cassidy shrank back a little further. Timothy, clever enough to see what was happening but not clever enough to save himself, stood next to her, stiff and sad and lonely, wanting to follow Katie but knowing that it would do no good. Something very shining had come into his life for a little while, and something very shining was going out. Very shining, and probably very dangerous.

He looked down at the top of his mother's head. She was smaller than he had ever remembered her. Magic had gone out of the room, and only the witch in the wood was left. Poor old witch.

Almost instinctively, he put his hand on her shoulder, but still he didn't say anything. When he looked up again, Octavia was standing in front of him, the last of the five Thornes to leave the Cassidy house.

"So sorry," said Octavia, lifting a languid tea-party hand, bent elegantly at the wrist. He might have reached for it, saved face by bowing back with equal elegance, bending from the waist, clicking his heels, but the thought never even occurred to him. He stood there as awkward as a lamb in April.

Octavia's heart gave a sudden little ache. Poor dear young man, bereft of his bride-to-be, his bright-star Katie, his new-found love. And he was made for loving, she thought, with that rumpled hair and that sweet upper lip. She studied him with her summer-blue eyes, making him look into hers and holding him so for a long moment before he looked away. Then, *Why not?* she thought. Dear young man, it would do him a world of good.

And Octavia, who believed so firmly in the education of dear young men, touched this one softly on the shoulder, and, in her turn, she left the Cassidy house, light of foot and kind of heart.

Timothy did not move, but Mrs. Cassidy drew a deep breath. "At last!" she said. In a moment, she would conquer this strange sensation of shrinking, uncomfortable like her bad leg but located differently. "Timothy, you are a very lucky . . ."

"Mother," said Timothy, "please be quiet."

Ten ∾

Katie did not appear at the breakfast table, the next morning, and the boarders missed her before the family did. Mr. Hermitage was especially indignant. Being a man who was addicted to changelessness in everything, he expected the Thornes to remain, changelessly, all in one place.

"She's run away again," he said accusingly.

"She did *not* run away," Mama told him for the tenth time.

"She ran off."

"She went to get married."

"Which she didn't do," said Mr. Hermitage and helped himself to more jam, which he spread thickly on the butter which he had already spread thickly on the toast.

Mama, who was used to letting men have the last word

if they needed it, nodded. Sweetened by jam and victory, Mr. Hermitage ate his way through two eggs and another piece of toast, this one with honey. He then rose from the table, patted at his moustache and said that he must be off on his workaday rounds.

As the door closed behind him, life resumed—spurts and murmurs of conversation, a handing about of plates, a pastoral sound of chewing. Of the three remaining boarders, two were stout and sober, with a Tweedledee combing of their scant hairs and a Tweedledum look to their buttons. The third was lank and agile, with rusty eyebrows and a loud laugh.

Tweedledee said brightly that Katie would undoubtedly turn up in time for lunch. Tweedledum agreed and reached for the jampot that Mr. Hermitage had vacated.

"I don't know," Mama said. "It's very distressing at breakfast time. Lunch, yes. Katie often misses lunch." She looked at Dawn, who was another one who often missed lunch, and added, "I know it's foolish to worry, but she has been so odd lately. . . ."

Dawn said, "I'll go find her, Mama. She's probably gone off to commune with herself. You can't commune at this breakfast table."

Mama agreed. "Well," she said, "we must just go right on as if nothing has happened."

But nothing has, thought the three boarders, and, beginning to feel somewhat out of touch, they folded their napkins carefully, rose to their feet, wished their hostesses well, and departed on their business of keeping the world on its even keel.

It was Dawn's reasonable assumption that Katie would be out in the woods, since woods are private places. Once inside them, however, Dawn forgot what she had come for. She was a natural and amazed student of all the natural and amazing world beyond her doorstep, and she dawdled now, stuffing bits of moss into her pocket, chewing on twigs, poking happily around burrowing places. It was pure chance when, drifting around the trunk of a very old, very wild cherry tree, cloud-gazing, leaf-gazing, she almost fell over the object of her search.

"Sorry," said Katie.

Dawn looked down at her. Katie's expression was that of a very intense young owl; her white forehead was furrowed with thinking, and her chin was set. Having apologized for being stepped on, she rubbed her nose and scowled straight ahead.

Dawn slid to the ground beside her and leaned against the rough bark, pleasant to feel between her shoulder blades. "Mama was anxious about you."

"I doubt it," said Katie.

Dawn somewhat doubted it too. "Well, Mr. Hermitage was anxious."

Katie said, "Mr. Hermitage has a wife already."

Dawn's eyebrows feathered upwards. After a moment, she said cautiously, "I don't think he was planning to propose to you, dear."

"Of course not," said Katie gloomily. "No one does." She then brightened suddenly, as if a shaft of sunlight had struck her, and made such a grandiloquent gesture that Dawn ducked just in time. "I've been thinking," she said, "about my life. I got started wrong."

"You did?" said Dawn, sounding faintly bemused.

"I don't mean getting born," Katie explained hastily. "That was all right. I mean, of late. That is," she added, in helpful translation, "recently."

85

Dawn nodded. She hoped it was the right response.

"And so," Katie went on, "I've been thinking—"

"You said that."

"I know, but I wasn't sure that you were listening."

"Oh, Katie, of course I was listening! That's what I came here for."

Katie turned and gave her a smile of real love and appreciation. "That was very nice of you, Dawn," she said gratefully. "I thought you came to tell me that I should have been at breakfast."

No, said Dawn, she hadn't come for that. She then said, very quietly, that the conversation seemed to be bogging down. Could they start again?

"Yes," said Katie, and did so. "I was thinking, and I came to a decision. I decided that Falling Grove was the wrong place to start my quest."

"Your *what?*"

"My quest. For a husband. And—" She held up her hand to ensure silence— "that is why I said I got started wrong."

"I see." Dawn pushed her hair back from her brow to give it air. "So your plan is to start all over again?"

Katie nodded vehemently. "Yes. But not in Falling Grove. Because Falling Grove was not the right place to start my quest." She paused. "I said that before too, didn't I?"

"I wasn't going to mention it."

"You're very good to me, Dawn. I'll miss you." Katie sighed. "I'll miss all of you."

"Are you leaving us?"

"But that's what I've been telling you," Katie said impatiently. "I'm leaving tomorrow morning—before sunrise." She sat up straight, apple-blossom cheeks, and

86

green eyes seeing visions. "I won't be gone long, just until I find a husband, and then I'll come right back here. Don't tell anybody, will you?"

"But they're sure to notice."

"I mean, don't tell them tonight. Tell them at breakfast time. And then you can tell everyone, even the boarders and Mr. Porter. For all of me," she said, sounding suddenly fierce, "you can tell the whole wide world, including Timothy Cassidy and that mother of his, too!"

Dawn reached out a hand and patted her sister's knee. There was a very long silence, during which the sun filtered through the old cherry's shade and the growing things in the ground could be heard to grow. Dawn broke it. "Well—"

"Don't argue," said Katie. "My mind is made up." She patted the hand that had patted her. "And don't worry. Because, this time, I have a real plan. I know exactly what I'm going to do." She jumped to her feet. "Dawn—"

"Yes, Katie?"

"Don't miss me," Katie said. "I'll be home very soon."

"—with a husband," Dawn said resignedly.

"Yes."

"And with Noah too, I have no doubt. And an Ark, of course." Dawn shook her head. "Well, if it takes longer than you expect, Katie love, send me a letter." The corners of her mouth curled upwards. "On second thought," said Dawn, "send me a dove."

Eleven ✒

Her mind made up, its corners firmly tucked in, Katie slept so soundly that the first wave of birdsong never reached her at all. It was not until an early crow screeched past her window, black and raucous with anger, that she woke to a rising sun.

She leaped out of bed. Her bag for travelling (not Dawn's suitcase, but a heavy gray piece of good stuff with twine around its neck) had been packed the night before, and there was nothing left for her to do but to wash and dress, at clockwork speed, in a sleeping household. Once ready to her own satisfaction, she opened the blinds (in case of sunshine), closed the window (in case of storms), and took a final look in her mirror.

The Cassidy Katie, she of the wrenched-back hair and downcast eyes, would not be going on this journey at all. The mirror gave her back a portrait of dews and brambles, of loose-swinging hair and eager green eyes. She spun triumphantly in the middle of the shabby carpet, then snatched up her bag, and flew moth-quiet down the backstairs. If there had been a banister, she would have slid.

In the kitchen, she gulped milk and gnawed bread before she let herself out the door and set off down the road.

As she walked, she swung her bag and sang. The Lord had seen fit to give Katie a lark's voice and a donkey's ear, and her song was as clear and loud as it was tuneless. When she came to the sign that marked the edge of Falling Grove, she subdued her general hallelujah and then stopped it altogether. Crossing her fingers for luck, she stepped over the line and entered the town like a child playing tag.

She was now on her way to meet her fate. If she did not meet him on the main street of Falling Grove, she intended to march on until she did, straight through the town and out the other side. It was only a matter of being resolute, and she repeated like a charm the words, "The first man I meet, the first man I meet."

The first man, however, was stout and beery, even from a distance. He had red whiskers, and he was walking on frantic tiptoes, trying to keep his balance on an invisible tightrope. Katie gave him one quick look and ducked up the nearest sidepath, waiting for him to stagger on past and so, technically, not meeting him at all. When he was safely gone by, she re-emerged and almost walked into a junkman's cart with a threadbare horse and a seedy driver.

She knew James the Junkman, who had an acquaintance with anybody's junk, and she knew him to be already married, so he didn't count. She stopped him with a raised hand. "Are you going my way?" she said sweetly, and, before he could answer, she had bounded lightly up onto the seat beside him.

He gazed at her speechlessly. In thirty-odd years of other people's castoffs and a good living out of them, nothing like this had ever happened to James the Junkman. He knew all about the Thorne family, of course—a junkman's rounds are as fruitful as a party line—and he thought highly of Clovelly, a young woman who understood good value in old iron and who could drive a bargain as hard and straight as she hammered nails. He respected Clovelly for her mastery of manly arts, had seen very little of Mama, thought Dawn and Octavia uncommonly easy to look at, and, at the safe distance of age and marital status, had fallen head over heels in love with Katie from the moment he set eyes on her.

Up until now, he had never passed more than a greeting, but she had sometimes crossed his dreams at night, causing him to kick his wife in bed, though without malice.

Now, when the dream appeared so suddenly out of nowhere and leaped to share the narrow seat of his cart, it had an appalling effect. This was not altogether James's fault. The dawn had been exceptionally rosy-fingered, and what was left of it seemed to be clinging to Katie in a very disturbing way. In addition to this, his elderly carthorse had been proceeding at a trot that was quite out of character, its ears set at a giddy angle. Finally, the collection of junk in his cart already included a very salable set of bedsprings. It was all too much. James's head whirled.

Katie, who was enjoying the altitude of the high seat, looked down at the world around her with extreme graciousness and gave a bounce of pleasure. The horse, filled with its mysterious vigor, trotted faster, and James stared between its ears and listened to his own heart, which was giving very odd thumps. The reins, like his jaw, hung slack.

They clopped their way, the three of them, straight through the town and out the other side. As the sun rose higher, Katie's sense of adventure diminished a little, and she began to feel faintly bored. Coming from a family which enjoyed creating situations if there were none at hand, she was not used to boredom, and James, though a good provider of transportation, was a silent man. She smothered a yawn politely, glanced sideways to see what if anything was going on in that silent head, and caught him looking from the corner of one eye. She smiled. It seemed the friendly thing to do.

James goggled. The friendly smile had tipped up the corners of a mouth that was certainly very—that was certainly—that was . . . He swallowed so hard he nearly choked, and Katie turned full around and gazed at him in real concern.

Eyes, thought James, not the first man to drown.

"It's the dust," Katie said kindly.

Not normally a religious man, James thought first of angels, and then he thought of other things. He swiveled his head, refreshing his memory of that smile, and was at once refreshed to the point of recklessness. He clucked at his horse, and, as the cart bounced to a faster rhythm, he took his right hand away from the reins and placed it, very deliberately, on Katie's knee. To steady her, of course.

She removed his right hand and gave it back to him.

He did not want it back but he made immediate use of it, pulling sharply on the gee rein and turning horse and cart into a small side road. Full of trees. Lined with bushes. Oh, very pleasant. The horse clopped, slowed, ambled. James was all ashake.

"Wherever are you going?" Katie inquired.

"Nowhere," he said wildly. It was not really his fault—this young Pan inside a middle-aged sack with Venus on the seat beside him. Better men than James have got themselves into trouble for worse reasons. "Thought we'd just get out and s-sit ourselves down on the road. You know?" He winked, poor dear.

"Oh," said Katie, demure as a wren, folding her hands, not moving. "I thought you'd be driving at least as far as the next town."

"Later," James said. "We're only young once, Katie." He poked her in the ribs with his elbow. "You know what I mean?"

She figured she did, but, along with the morning air and the feeling of adventure, she could feel a small devil rising inside her. The look she turned on James was as pure as sunlight. She widened her eyes, and one white hand stole forth to touch his coatsleeve timidly. "But you're a married man," she said, in a voice that trembled with innocence.

For just a moment, the touch of that little hand almost undid him, and he thought he ought to turn the horse and cart around and take this flowerlike girl straight home. But then he remembered Katie's family connections, and he was able to master his foolish thoughts. "What's my being married got to do with it?" he said.

"Oh!" said Katie, and she took her little hand away from his coatsleeve and pressed it to her heart. "You mean that you want to leave your wife and marry *me?*" She looked up at the sky. It was nice and blue.

James's jaw came unhinged again. "Who said anything about leaving my wife?"

"You don't want to marry me?" She drooped, beginning to enjoy herself very much.

Promise her anything, he thought. "I do, Katie, I do!" he cried.

"Oh, James. You *would* leave your wife for me?"

"I'd leave anything for you," said the great god Pan, and he reached out, reeling with dizziness, for the slender waist and the moist mouth and those green, green eyes.

Katie slipped sideways, downwards and out, and she flowed to the ground in one silky movement. James threw down the reins and leaped to follow her. The woods were bright with dryads, and there was a ringing of cloven hooves. With a splendid snort, he plunged toward his dream.

He missed. The Mooncalf could have told him how it was done.

He plunged once more. Katie darted behind the cart, light and cold as a snowflake, dodged to the other side, and jumped lightly up onto the high seat. Over her shoulder, she waved a cheerful farewell, then she gathered up the reins and clucked at the horse. It broke into its disloyal trot, and the cart lurched off merrily down the road.

It took James a full minute to realize what had happened, since he was not by nature a ready man and a lifetime of easy junkdealing and vague domesticity had done little enough to sharpen his wits. Now, total awareness dawned on him very slowly, as horse, cart, bedsprings, and beauty receded into a distance that was dim with dust and sun.

He raised his fist and struck the air and shouted, "Katie!

Come back here!" He dropped his fist and wailed, "Katie, come back!" The bushes around him shook with laughter, and a mocking echo said Katie-come-Katie-come-Katie. James thrust his hands deep into his pockets, gulped hard, and swore that he would never forgive her.

And he never did, but he never forgot her either.

Twelve ✺

Twenty minutes away and well down the road, Katie turned the
horse loose, with the reins knotted on its docile neck and a
friendly whack on its rump. It trotted off briskly enough,
then looked back, found that it was a free agent and set to
a peaccable cropping of the roadside grass.

It would go home in its own good time, and James,
swearing and mightily relieved, would find it there. It was
his own fault, Katie told herself, and the faint gleam of
repentance that crossed her mind flickered out very comfortably.

She stood gazing around, not quite certain of her where-
abouts. The town of Falling Grove was behind her, the sun
was climbing, and the road that stretched ahead was
dusty, empty and bright. She shrugged and set out, but a

half hour's sturdy walking brought no encounters of any kind, much less potential husbands, and it began to look as if the road planned to go on forever, straight as a string and headed for limbo.

She was now on the far side of Falling Grove where she had never ventured, and, being all new, it should have been interesting, but, being all unpeopled, it was profoundly dull. She found herself merely putting one foot in front of the other, close to plodding, and she began to wonder if the whole venture—perish the thought—had been a mistake. At this moment of pessimism, the road started to rise, and with it Katie's spirits.

It rose abruptly until there was nothing but sky at the top of the next hill, and then another hill beyond that. The sun got hotter. The dust did not settle. Katie, who was perhaps something of an extremist, had just reached a state of mind where she would willingly trade her soul, her body, and her prospects of a wedding ring for one cool draught of plain water, when the last hill crested.

Not far below her, stretched in enticing view, lay a valley of woods and farm land. Next to her, perched at the brow of the hill and no more than a few yards off the road, sat a square, functional little building, with a weather-beaten sign swinging in front of it.

When she came nearer, she saw that the sign said GRO-CERIES BEER and that the door of the building was ajar. There was a large front window, full of dusty glass bottles, a pile of brown bags, several seedy-eyed potatoes, and what appeared to be a sprinkling of flour over everything. In an instantaneous survey, Katie redesigned the window display, married the shop's owner, and moved her family into the neighborhood. Hope was as reviving as water.

She touched her hair, lifted her round chin, fixed a winning smile on her lips, and stepped over the threshold.

The interior was dark and unwelcoming, combining dust and damp with an overlay of licorice. A counter ran across the back of the room, branches of dried dill hung from the ceiling, and the walls were lined with empty shelves.

Katie cleared her throat. A head, which had been resting on folded arms, raised itself from the counter. Female, thought Katie with sincere disappointment.

A throaty, disobliging voice said, "You want something?"

Katie marched across the floor, straight to the counter, and planted herself. The owner of the voice looked up, and brown eyes like pebbles stared into green eyes like emeralds. Kate said, rather belligerently, "My name is Katie Thorne."

"Pleased," said the voice indifferently. "Mine's Emma Swann." There was a pause. "Mrs. Emma Swann yesterday, Mrs. Emma Nobody today." Emma Nobody had a face like soft wax, and she was neither goodlooking nor homely, neither young nor old. The only thing you could say about her for sure was that she had been pulled through a knothole.

"What happened yesterday?" Katie asked. "Can I have a drink?"

Emma leaned her cheek on her fist. "There ain't been beer in this dump since last Christmas."

"I don't want beer. I just want some water."

"Pump's out back."

Katie shrugged and went out back, through the slit of a back door that let in a streak of light. The pump creaked like a donkey and the water flowed brown, but after a session with the pumphandle it came clear. Katie doubled over to turn her mouth up to its spill, and came out, gasping and choking but quenched. She took extra time, washed her face and hands, got a comb out of her travel bag and, after a minute, shook out her hair and braided it, cool and neat but not skinned tight.

She went back in. Emma had put her head down into her arms again. Katie said, "Is there anything to eat?" and the head came up. Emma made a large inclusive gesture. "Help yourself," she said. "It's all mine, lock, stock and barrel. It's what he married me for, and he c'n whistle for it. And, if he comes here after what isn't his, I'll blow his head off. With a gun," she added specifically.

Katie took the top off a crock and peered inside. Something, spiders, mold. She put the top on, opened another and found a large lump of brown sugar, like a rock, which she took out and began to lick. Emma watched for a moment, bit her thumbnail, and sighed. "If you're really hungry, there's biscuits in a sack."

Katie said, thank you, she wasn't really hungry, but she was fond of sugar. "You've got troubles?" she said sympathetically.

"I had one," Emma said. "I ditched him last night."

"Your husband?"

Emma gave a short, buzzsaw laugh. "My husband, all right, but he's got no claims. He could put me in a sack and stuff me down a drainpipe, he's still got no claims. Such as it is, and it sure ain't much, the store's mine." The pebble eyes brightened. "You want a job?"

"I'm not looking for a job," Katie said. "I'm looking for a—" She stopped, feeling this was not the ideal audience for a discussion of marriages. Also, even if Mr. Swann had not been already a husband (an abandoned husband), he did not seem to be promising matrimonial material.

"I don't blame you," Emma said. "I haven't any money to pay you with, anyway. It's just that I'd like some company that isn't a man. Him and his three brothers, you can have 'em all."

"Three brothers?" Katie said quickly, and then, not to sound greedy, she added, "I've got three sisters."

"Tell 'em not to marry," said Emma.

"It's not a marrying household, except for—" Again she got that far and no farther.

"Glad to hear it. The Swanns ain't either, but Eben wanted to own the store, and I came with it. If he tries to take over, I'll shoot his head off."

Katie nodded, the threat sounding more cordial than bloodthirsty. "His brothers' heads, too?"

"No, just Eben. He's the ape."

"What are the others like?" Katie inquired, doing research.

"Well, the two youngest are skinny and kind of dumb. The second one isn't bad at all." She considered this for a moment, and then added, "But no juice."

"Like Timothy," Katie said, without meaning to have said anything.

"Probably," said Emma. "Sure you won't stay?"

She said, yes, she was sure, but then she lingered. After a moment, she offered, almost shyly, "But I could help you clean things up a bit before I go, if you'd like. The window maybe? It's full of flour."

"Bug powder."

"Oh. I'm sorry."

"Well, they're friendly."

There was a vague silence. Katie, thinking the matter over, began to consider a postponement of her journey, at least for a few days. She found herself rather liking this barn of a room, with its odd smells and its many shelves, and there was no reason why possible husbands might not come to this store as well as anywhere. "I could stay a while, if you want—" she began.

"No," said Emma, "I don't want. I've changed my mind. I'm pleased to have you offer, but I don't want." A smile spread slowly across the soft-wax face. "I'm queen of the castle, Katie Thorne, I'm free. I'm as good as single. When my bones get over being tired, I'll be the happiest female thing in the world. A woman's a fool to get married."

Katie stared at her, just this side of glaring. "I," she said resentfully, "am going to get married."

Emma shrugged. "Free country."

Just managing not to stamp, Katie turned on her heel and stalked out the door. She squared her shoulders, straightened her back and once more set her feet firmly on the road to matrimony, where they belonged.

From behind her, Emma called out "Katie!" and her voice was as clear and merry as a blackbird's. Katie spun around, bristling, and there was Emma, standing in her own doorway and waving a cheerful farewell.

The devil with her! thought Katie, who never swore. Then suddenly she laughed, waved back as she would wave to a sister, and went on down the road, feeling better. After all, some were lucky in marriage and some were not. Katie Thorne was going to be one of the lucky ones.

Once down the hill, she set herself to looking for the Swann farm. Off to the east (west?), she could see houses clustering together, and she pictured them all respectable, with stiff faces and tight gardens and narrow paths that led to narrow doorways. Off to the west (east?), she could see a green copse of little trees and big bushes, set into a green meadow.

Where there was a meadow, she told herself, there would be a farm, and where there was a farm, there would be a farmhouse. And in that farmhouse, according to logic and presentiment, there would be four brothers named Swann, three of them not taken and all of them needing a woman's hand.

She headed for the meadow with a very springy step, almost running, and waded straight into the deep warm grass. It rose up to clutch her ankles and knees, and it smelled of weeds and honey. Dawn would have sat down to play with it, but Dawn's sister strode through like a farmer's wife.

The house almost leaped up at her out of the landscape. It was a queer shape for a farmhouse, its windows too small, its roof too big, and its elbows sticking out. The plum color outside clashed furiously with the red of the barn beyond, but Katie chose to look upon it all with a kindly eye. It was probably her future home.

She marched up the front steps crisply and whacked on the plum door. The sound went into the house and came out empty. She whacked again, and still got nothing but hollowness.

"Looking for someone, miss?" said a man's voice behind her.

Thirteen ∽

Katie spun around so fast she bit her tongue.

Standing on the bottom step, flashing a smile at her, big as a bear and brawny as an oak tree, was the handsomest man she had ever seen. He was a brassy sunset, leaning there against the porch railing; a trumpet. Compared to the Mooncalf, and Timothy, and James the Junkman, this one was an emperor.

"Looking for someone, miss?" he said again, bold eyes and melting butter.

He couldn't be the ape, and dumb-and-skinny he certainly was not; so he had to be the fourth brother, the one Emma had called not bad at all. She stared at him in wide-eyed appreciation.

He blinked for a second, but his smile got broader. "Cat got your tongue?"

"I bit it," Katie said coolly, recollecting that she had seen handsome men before now. "Would this be the Swann farm?"

"You want it to be, lady," he said enthusiastically, "that's what it is." He then added, "Yes, ma'am, it's the Swann farm," suddenly all tame cat.

Katie smiled a little inward smile. He must be the second brother all right, and she could see that what Emma called "no juice" was really shyness. It wasn't the first time a big man had got tangled in his own feet around a Thorne. She studied him attentively, and then said, "There's four of you."

He looked puzzled, and his jaw went a little slack, but he nodded.

Standing there, two steps above him, she folded her arms and heard with pleasure the sound of her own voice, smooth and firm as the custards she had wasted on Mrs. Cassidy. A casual bystander might have said that the voice didn't go with the green eyes and the bright cheeks and the ruffled look of a meadow in a warm breeze, but the only bystander around wasn't that casual. "You're looking for a housekeeper," Katie informed him briskly.

"We are?" He thought a moment. "Yeah, I guess that's what we're looking for all right." He rubbed his chin and added, "Ours left us," as if he had just realized something.

"I've been housekeeper at a lot of places," Katie said. "One of them was a mansion. Six servants under me," she noted dreamily.

He knew she was lying, and she knew that he knew, which made everything very simple. He swung up the steps in one easy stride, picked up her travel bag, and pushed open the plum-colored door. "You're hired," he said. "What's your name?"

"Thorne," said Katie. "Katharina Thorne." She walked into the house ahead of him. "What's yours?"

"Eben Swann."

Eben was the one that Emma was married to. Katie's mouth fell open. ("Catching flies, love?" Mama would have said, Mama who was always unsurprised.) She took a deep breath, swallowed her shock, and resigned herself to the fact that she could not marry this one, since he had a wife already, though holed up on a hill. On the other hand, if Emma could describe this handsome creature as an ape, then the two she called skinny and dumb were probably as fat as butter-jars and had knife-edge brains. As for the second brother, who was juiceless . . . Katie's eyebrows arched in anticipation.

"Where you going?" said Eben.

"Into the kitchen," Katie told him, finding that was where she was. The house must have been built back to front so you could watch the cows from the parlor. It was an enormous kitchen, square and high. On the stove, something in a stewpot was wrinkling the air with a gamy smell and making steam curl toward the ceiling. Her nose counted onions three times over, turnips or parsnips with the dirt still on them, and some kind of meat that she couldn't even guess at. The kitchen was messy, but it was mostly top mess, like grease spilled on the wood table, and Katie guessed that Emma had kept house better than she kept store. Maybe that was why she was liking the store now, Katie thought and vaguely understood.

She stood looking around her and said abruptly, "Where's the parlor?"

"What do you want a parlor for?"

She clicked her tongue impatiently, and he shrugged his wide shoulders and said, "It's full of junk."

"What kind of junk?"

"Pigs feet, bears ears, kindling and spit."

"We'll air it out," said Katie, very sweetly. "Where are your brothers?"

"What do you care?"

"I like to see who I'm working for," she said.

He grunted. "Who told you about us?"

"Mama," said Katie inspired. "Where's *my* room?"

He started to say something and then changed his mind, and just at that moment the front door opened and shut with a creak and a bang, and there was a sound of large boots in the hallway. The man who was in the boots stopped in the kitchen doorway and sucked in his breath. He was close to being as handsome as Eben, but he was only middling tall and middling broad, and his mouth, at the moment, was slightly ajar. Eyes and mouth both widened, the way a child's might, but then his face firmed up and he gave a kind of laugh and made a bow that was almost graceful. Only, he made it to his brother. "That was real quick, Eben," he said.

Eben scowled. "She's a housekeeper."

"Looks like one, for sure."

"And it's a dirty house," said Katie. She, who had never minded boots trailing through the house at Falling Grove, gave him a glare that should have caked the mud on his. "Take your boots off," she told him.

"*My* boots?"

"It's *my* kitchen floor," said Katie, feeling they might as well get used to the idea. She then raised her green, green eyes to his, and gave him an utterly trusting smile.

He gulped. "Eben's got *his* on," he said lamely.

Eben gave a yelp of laughter. Katie transferred her smile to him, and there was a long moment of nothing said.

This time, it was the back door that opened, and the two other Swann brothers tramped through the front of the house and into the kitchen—four more boots, but not so heavy as the first four. Katie looked the newcomers over critically—dumb they might be, skinny they were. If you stood them sideways, they'd disappear. Both had button eyes, mouths big enough to hook over their ears, and round heads on pipestem necks. The only thing they had in common with their kin was that they too stared.

Katie stared back calmly, her hands clasped lightly in front of her, fingers laced, her expression judicious. It didn't take long to make up her mind. Eben was out of the running—married already, although his wife had walked out on him. The skinny ones were out of the running, too; between them, they would just about prop up a peavine. But the middle one would do very well indeed.

She looked at him now, until he blinked the way Eben had, and then she said to all of them, pleasantly, "Next time, wipe your feet on the doormat before you come inside."

One of the skinny ones said, "We don't have a doormat, miss."

"Get one," said Katie.

He looked uncertainly toward Eben. "Is she moving in?"

"I am," said Katie.

"Are we paying her?" He was still talking to Eben.

"Of course, you're paying me," said Katie, also talking to Eben.

"Room and board," Eben said, not taking his eyes off her.

"Room and board and wages," said Katie.

He started to say no, and then he winked at the middle brother and said yes. At least, she thought that was the one he winked at, although she couldn't be sure. It didn't matter all that much anyway, because as soon as the middle one was married to her, he would become the head of the house, instead of Eben. That was what having a wife did for a man, and perhaps that was why Noah had been so firm about marriage as an institution. This thought came to Katie as something of a revelation, and she recognized its usefulness at once.

"What's your name?" said Katie, addressing her intended husband.

"Adam. Adam Swann."

Adam was the next best name to Noah. She was extremely gratified—half a day away from home, and already finding the house, the man, and the future, while standing in a strange kitchen. She sniffed the air, and the stew on the stove smelt better than it had when she came in. It was past noon and she was hungry and, she thought philosophically, you can get used to anything.

"You may show me to my room," she said to Adam, rather grandly.

Eben jerked his head to indicate who was boss in the house. "Give her Emma's."

Emma had a room all to herself, then. So why did she choose to live at the back of a draggletailed store, with the floor for a bed and the bugs for friends? Katie shot a quick look at Eben, and then she shadowed it with her long soft lashes. Eben's face was blacker than a black thundercloud.

She guessed that Emma hadn't been able to manage him, but she knew that she, Katie, could manage anybody. Giving Eben a scant nod, she let Adam lead the way out of what was now her kitchen, and she followed him up the stairs, just as she had once followed Timothy Cassidy. These stairs were wider, it being a wider house. Draughty in winter time, no doubt, but she was used to draughts, and the Swann house had many desirable features.

She stepped into her new room with what, given a less light foot, would have been a solid thump of possession. It was a pleasant enough place, with a certain amount of comfort—a good chair to sit on and curtains made of some thin bright goods. The only thing on the top of the bureau was a small clock. It was lying on its side, and Katie went over and picked it up. It was not ticking, so she wound it carefully. Perhaps Emma had meant to take it with her. Perhaps, one of these days, she ought to take it up the hill to Emma. A ticking clock would make good company in a lonesome hole.

But Emma doesn't want company, thought Katie, so clearly that it was almost as if she had said it out loud. It was even possible that Emma had known very well how to handle Eben, but just got tired of doing it. Handling men was not all that difficult, once you got the trick. Katie sighed.

"Trouble?" said Adam.

Up here in the small room, he looked bigger than he had downstairs. When she didn't answer, he said "Trouble?" again, stepped close, and slid an arm around her waist.

She spun free with the ease of infinite practice, and he stood for a moment with his arm curved to a waist and holding nothing. "You can go now," she said calmly, and turned her back on him.

He said, "Well—" heavily, and then, after a while, he said, "Are you really a housekeeper?"

She was opening drawers, peering inside and then closing them again. "Yes," she said, "I am," and added, "One time I had ten servants under me," upping the head count slightly for effect.

He gaped. His brother Eben had not believed even six servants, but his brother Eben was bigger, brighter and bolder. For the second time, Katie sighed.

"Ten," Adam said, not making a question of it.

"Twelve, actually," Katie said casually, "but it sounds like bragging."

"You'd make somebody a good wife," said Adam.

This was quicker than she had looked for. She turned around and found that he was sitting on Emma's bed and patting the counterpane. "You're flighty," he said. "Come and sit by me."

She stayed where she was. His remark about wives had evidently been more an observation than a proposal of marriage, but it showed he could think along the right lines.

"Eben's got a wife," Adam said.

She started to tell him she knew that already, but she said "Oh?" instead.

"She walked out on him." He waited for a reaction, got none, and went on. "She was a fair enough cook, but she could skin you with her tongue. I warned Eben not to marry, the Swanns aren't marrying men. If you think about it," he added, "marriage is against nature." When she directed the full glare of her green eyes at him, he pulled in his chin. "Well, I guess it's all right for women," he conceded.

Katie shrugged. He had a mind that would be easy to change, and she had plenty of time to change it for him. "You can go now," she said.

"Me?" He laughed, rooster-crowing but not quite that certain a rooster.

"You," said Katie.

He stared for a moment, and then he got up and left. She closed the door on his departing heels.

Smiling to herself placidly, she yawned and stretched. Starting with James, the day had been an active one, and the bed looked tempting. She wandered over to sit on it, bounced, found it acceptable and contemplated a nap. Then she decided she was hungry first and sleepy second. Humming softly, she strayed to Emma's bureau, gazed briefly but with satisfaction into the cloudy mirror, and began to unbraid her hair.

It was hanging to her waist when she heard the door-knob rattle behind her, and she turned to find the entire doorway filled with six-foot-two of Eben Swann.

"Katharina," Eben said, leaning on the jamb. "What do they call you at home?"

"Katharina." Her eyes were measuring just how much space there was in the doorway that he wasn't filling. Plenty, for slipping past. She yanked her hair back from her face, like Mrs. Cassidy's Katie MacPherson, and began to braid it, quick and tight.

"Not Katie? not Kitty?" Eben said. "Not pretty Kitty?"

Too bad she'd sent Adam away. Eben was a big man, but not big enough to be mild. For the third time, she sighed, and this sigh—although she could not know it—was the sister of Dawn's sigh when she bit the sales-man. The salesman had been a big man too.

"Katharina." She repeated it evenly and started toward the door.

"Going somewhere?" said Eben.

"Downstairs."

"Are you? Are you, pretty Kitty?" He took his shoulder away from the jamb and straightened up leisurely.

There was still space on the further side of him, and Katie went through it—not hastily, but with the beautiful swiftness of a swallow arrowing into a cliff hole. She skimmed down the stairs and headed straight for the kitchen, for Adam whom she intended to marry, and for the two skinny brothers who would soon be her in-laws.

Adam was sitting on the kitchen table, with one boot off and one boot on. The two skinny ones were hunched on the bench, leaning slightly together so their shoulders touched. Needed each other to hold each other up, Katie thought scornfully, crossed to the stove, and took a stir of the stew in the kettle.

Eben was right behind her. He strode through the room as if he and she were the only ones in it. He took her by the shoulders and pulled her against him, nose squashed on the front of his rough wool shirt.

She did not care for the front of his rough wool shirt, nor for his big confident paws, nor for getting her nose squashed. She pulled away, her spoon dripping grease on the floor, and looked toward Adam. He got off the table, boot dangling from his hand, and said in a cautious voice, "Now, Eben—" When nothing happened, he cleared his throat and said, "Now, Eben—" again. Then he moved away to the other side of the kitchen. After a short silence, his two skinny brothers joined him.

Eben laughed and straddled the bench they had vacated. He stood there, crooking a finger at Katie, grinning at her with the whitest teeth of any man in the world. "Come on over to me, Kitty," he said. "You come on over."

"I will!" said Katie, and she came, like a whirlwind. She charged straight at him, arms stiff, head down. She hit his chest with her hands out flat and her strong wrists behind them—Silly fool, strutting above a bench that would trip him like a tree-root, a jackass to be knocked over by his own conceit.

A man who is being regarded as an off-balance jackass is

at a disadvantage in a situation of this kind. Eben went over backwards with a crash that shook the kitchen beams.

Adam gawked. The two skinny brothers made little dry sounds, like little dry peas rattling in a pod. Eben, flat on his back, raised himself on his elbows, stared at her for one astonished moment, and then suddenly let out a roar of laughter. He sounded like a spring bull.

Katie whirled, snatched up her travel bag from the table where she had left it, and shot out of the kitchen, through the hall, across the porch, and down the steps.

In the beat of ten seconds, Eben was up and after her, but he had more fat on him than there looked to be and more lead in his feet than the big leather boots told. Distance gulped up the girl he would never have, and the roar that came out of him, as he stood watching her get smaller and smaller in the distance, was no longer a roar of laughter.

Katie didn't look back, and it was a quarter of a mile before she even slowed down.

Fourteen ∞

By the time she was in open country again, she had her breath
back but not her self-esteem, and she walked the next mile
with her lower lip sticking out and a frown scratched
across her forehead. From time to time, she kicked a stone
out of her path or raised her head to glare at a passing
sparrow.

Eager as she was to go through life two by two, she was
forced to admit that she was making poor progress. Adam
Swann was no more her fate than Timothy Cassidy or the
Mooncalf, and it was no use brooding about it. She took
consolation in the memory of Eben Swann with his heels
tucked into his ears. Poor, poor Eben! she did sincerely
hope that he had landed very hard.

Cheered by the thought, she walked more briskly, but the next bend in the road was like all the others, and she was feeling a distinct emptiness that was neither fatigue nor unrequited love, but simple hunger. She began to regret the rejection of Emma's biscuits; even the memory of the Swanns' greasy stew evoked a melancholy yearning. She shook her head, tightened her belt, and set to walking faster. Left foot, right foot.

There was another bend, a hedge, a house. The house had dormer windows like eyebrows, a vine on its chimney, and a little girl on its tiny lawn. The little girl was as round as a ball of butter, and she was chewing a very large bun. She looked delicious, but not as delicious as the bun.

"Hello," said Katie, her mouth watering.

The child made a small noise, not quite a growl, gripped the bun more firmly and began to lick its surface. Sugar, thought Katie hostilely. "My name's Katie," she said, at her pleasantest. "Katie Thorne."

"I know," said the child.

"Oh, you do not!"

"I do, now."

The logic was unarguable. Katie, recognizing a natural enemy, put a wheedle into her voice. "What's *your* name, little girl?"

"Sugar Bun," said the little girl, and went on licking.

Serves me right, Katie thought fairly, and took direct action. Her hand flickered out, fast as a pickpocket, and she snatched the bun clean out of the fat clutching paws.

Sugar Bun roared instantly, a practiced roar, wide-mouthed, red-faced. Without a tremor of conscience, Katie once more fled from a scene of her own making. The roar became a bellow, and the heavens rang with the injustice of it all. There was a slamming of doors, a soothing of voices, which faded as Katie put a safe distance between herself and the swindled child.

The child was too fat, anyway.

With a placid smile, Katie raised the bun and took a large bite. Sugar frosted her lips, jam trickled down her chin. With a cry of pure joy, and holding her treasure tenderly so as not to drip down her front, she stepped off the roadway and into the green shade of a wide-branched tree. Sliding down on a pillow of soft grass, she surrendered herself to the occasion.

After a while, she licked her fingers, taking them one by one, in a slow cat contentment. Her head was cool in dappled shade, her toes were warm in gentle sun. An inner calm filled her, along with the bun . . . and the sugar . . . and the jam. . . .

When she opened her eyes again, the shadows were very long. It was getting dark, and she scrambled to her feet and took a look at the sky. The sun was not only low on the western horizon, but it was shrouded in heavy gray clouds. A breeze had crept into the air, and she could feel it between her shoulder blades, a little ferret with sharp mean teeth. It was going to rain any minute, and she had better find shelter.

Opening her travel bag, she pulled out the wool shawl she had crammed inside, tossed it over her shoulders and brought the ends together under her chin, then turned around calmly to survey her situation.

Lightning split the sky. Thunder turned it black. Katie gave a single yelp of protest and dived for the woods. A tree-trunk rose up and hit her, then spun her into a bush that tore at her shawl with briary fingers. No sooner had she ripped it loose than the ferret-wind snatched it away again.

She snatched it back valiantly, and the wind dropped at

once, giving her an idiotic moment of triumph, thinking she had won. All through the woods, the silence grew. Everything held still, and then, in a great rush of wild and wet, the rain came.

She was soaked in ten seconds. The trees were no shelter at all. When a thunderstroke shook the ground, the tree-trunks trembled, and she wished herself back on the road, picturing lightning running along the leaves and branches, surrounding her with fire, burning her to cinders. Or was she too wet to burn?

If I'm not burned up, I'll drown, she thought piteously, and longed for home. Her mother and her sisters flashed before her eyes, all of them dry. The storm gathered itself mightily—a cloudburst, a torrent, drenching her and the world around her in majestic impartiality.

Running would be useless, there was nowhere to run to. All she could do was to stay where she was, huddled, soaked, passive, her shawl clinging to her shivering body, her hair streaming, her eyes clenched as tight as her fists. Time went on forever.

At last, the storm dwindled. The thunder gave a faint satisfied growl as if, having eaten her, it could go away. The teeth of the wind barely nibbled. The rain became no more than a tiny dripping, like honey from a spoon. Katie opened her eyes.

A very faint glimmer of setting sun was creeping through the trees, polishing leaves, outlining pale raindrops on gold twigs. Slowly, a tottering convalescent, Katie unwound herself from her shawl. As a garment, it was now as useless as a woolly wet lamb, asking only to be carried.

She sneezed, rubbed the back of her hand across her nose, wondered how long it would take for her to die of general chills and disaster, and forgave her family and friends on her deathbed. She then stuck her chin out fiercely and began to walk.

For no more than fifty yards, she squelched her way. When the woods stopped, it was as sudden as if they had vanished into their own roots, and she stepped out into open land. Civilization. Houses.

She marched straight to the nearest door, raised her fist and pounded. Whether they wanted one or not, whoever lived here had a guest. If necessary, she was quite prepared to scream, shout or swoon on the front steps. She would become a waterfall, a weatherspout. She would flood the inhabitants out of their dens.

Her fist hit wood for the fourth time, and she was just making plans to break a window and climb through it, when the door opened.

Neat gray hair, done in a bun very like the late Katie MacPherson's, appeared on a level with Katie's chin. Katie's fist dropped, and she said, "Excuse me, ma'am," minding her manners politely now that she could see that whoever lived in this house was much too small to throw her out. "Excuse me, ma'am, I'm very wet."

The miniature lady had pale blue eyes in a round face that was feather-stitched with wrinkles. Her dress was as tidy as a primrose, and she looked distressingly alert, as if she had just stepped out of a wren-house. "Oh, you *are* wet!" she cried in a little fluty voice, and then she turned her head and called behind her. "Jeremy dear, could you come here for a moment?"

Katie stood still, but her heart leaped. Her heart knew at once who Jeremy was. He was *the* he, the husband for whom she had been searching. Why else had she come through fire and flood and perils, if not to be led to this very door? She hung poised, waiting for the step in the hallway.

The step was, more accurately, a shuffle. The head that came around the corner was framed in dandelion fluff, whiskers as round and milky as a cat's bowl.

Katie, smothering a wail, produced instead a fledgling's cry. Instantly, as if he had been wound up, the old gentleman began to cluck. Clucking, he gazed at her. His wife, which was what she must be, was the first to speak. "You're lost!" she exclaimed eagerly.

Katie hesitated. They were a very odd pair, and, in fact, she was now beginning to feel drowned in indoor sympathy, instead of outdoor rain. It all seemed a little too much, but the very excess found an echo within her. She lifted her chin, bravely, and she said, "I am not lost." Then, swaying slightly, a flower on a delicate stem, she added softly, "I *have* no home."

The old gentleman sprang to support her, but she waved him off. "No, no," she said. "I'm quite all right. It's just that—I've had nothing to eat all day but a tiny bun. . . ." This was not fair to the bun which had been quite large, and sugary as well, but the memory of the distant, beautiful object put an honest tremor into her voice. "If I could have just a mouthful of something—a crust—Then I could be on my way. . . ."

They both cried "Nonsense!" exactly as they were supposed to do. Mrs. Jeremy said, "I'll get you some soup," and vanished instantly. Mr. Jeremy, punctuating with clucks, said, "You'll catch your death of cold in those wet clothes. I'll get you a—a nightgown."

She gave him a smile that was all green eyes, and he said, "Yes, well—'hem" and rushed away. From the kitchen end of the house, there came a pleasing clatter of dishes.

118

Katie, left alone and in temporary possession, looked around the room. It was exactly like its owners, everything small and housely, knickknacks cunningly placed in corners that could have been empty, little mats on little tables. She had a feeling that if she moved she would knock something over, so, playing safe, she sat down on the nearest chair, pulled off her shawl and laid the wet-wool lamb across her lap.

"Here we are!" said Mrs. Jeremy, coming in from the kitchen and smelling divinely of hot soup. Beside the soup, on a tray, was thick white bread, and the bread was thick with yellow butter. Katie reached for it, and, for a space in time, there was only the sound of steady eating and the tick of a clock on the narrow mantelpiece between two china shepherdesses. Mrs. Jeremy, hands over her apron, stood and gazed. When her husband returned, with a nightgown over his arm, she took it from him and shooed him out of the room.

Katie's spoon struck bottom. Mrs. Jeremy held out the gown and said, "Take your things off, child, and put this on. Have you had enough to eat?—Oh dear, I forgot the cake, it's only a day old!"

She was off again. Katie stared after her for a moment, got up to put the tray on the nearest table (an odd little one with bowlegs ending in paws) and then slid unconcernedly out of her clothes.

"Oh dear!" said Mrs. Jeremy from the doorway, and vanished precipitately.

With her went the cake. Katie moved swiftly to pull on the nightgown, which was short but generously wide and certainly terribly cozy, and then called out urgently, "It's all right, ma'am."

The cake was as good as Octavia's, cloudlike, nourishing, shortlived. "Now," said Mrs. Jeremy, "we must tuck

you up into bed, because you'll need a good night's rest."
Abloom with kindness and determinedly tireless, she was
trotting about again, gathering up Katie's wet clothes,
saying she would dry them and tidy them, clucking like
her husband, ticking like the clock. Tick-cluck, tick-
cluck, tick-cluck. "Come along now, before you fall over."

Not at all resigned to going to bed just after sundown,
but full of food and suffocated in benevolence, Katie
thought it politic to give a wide yawn. "There!" Mrs.
Jeremy said triumphantly and led the way up the staircase,
through a hallway and into a little room with a little bed.
There were shepherdesses here too, a quilt with busy little
pink and white flowers, and a round rag rug that seemed
to have been starched by some too diligent hand. As a
room, it was either charming or insufferable, depending on
the point of view, but it was definitely an improvement on
being lost in a thundering forest.

The bed looked soft. "It's *so* pretty," Katie said, as if
one of the china shepherdesses had got inside her.

"It is, isn't it?" Cluck. "I'm only sorry that I can't let
you have the spare room, which is much bigger. But our
John is coming day after tomorrow, and of course we must
keep it ready for him."

Katie's ears pricked. "John?"

"Our youngest grandson." Mrs. Jeremy was busy turning back the quilt, there was another one underneath it,
less meadowy. "He's going to be staying with us for the
rest of the summer."

"John," said Katie, her eyes suddenly extremely green.
She was not by nature even a competent mathematician,
but her head had begun to do a very simple sum. "Your
grandson," she said, and after a moment, she added delicately, "He'd be—how old?"

120

"Twenty-one, last March."

Twenty-one. What a delightful age for a young man! Katie smiled.

Mrs. Jeremy nodded and smiled back. "He's very close to us, John is. I think I can say that he really feels this is his second home."

Katie said how sweet that was.

Mrs. Jeremy sighed. "My husband and I often think we should move to a smaller house, this is too large for the two of us. But then . . ."

"But then," said Katie astutely, "where would John go when he comes?"

"Exactly."

Katie gazed up at the ceiling. "It must be a great deal of work for you," she said, with the utmost consideration. "All the cleaning and the dusting and the mending, and then the cooking—for two men—in this big house. You really need another pair of hands, don't you?"

Mrs. Jeremy clucked.

Katie clucked.

"Of course," Mrs. Jeremy said, "my husband does what he can, but of course one knows that, although men *mean* well—"

"Oh, they do!"

"—they're still not quite . . ."

"Oh, they aren't!" said Katie.

"You're a very understanding child," Mrs. Jeremy told her, and went on talking fast as if she was used to being interrupted. "My dear Jeremy is more help than our dear John, who is very little help at all, I'm afraid. But then John is always studying."

Katie clucked again, finding this a very useful device. The situation had begun to unfold in a most delightful manner—John coming to stay, Mrs. Jeremy needing extra hands, Katie right there with a pair of them. She did not repeat her cluck, but she did almost coo.

"He studies too hard," Mrs. Jeremy said, and her sigh was half regret and half pride. "I *know* he studies too hard. I wish someone could take his mind off his books."

Well, thought Katie very sweetly, perhaps someone can.

Fifteen ❦

Katie's first view of John Taggit was from an upstairs window,
and her first observation was that his hair was very neat on
top. From this, she drew the instant conclusion that he
would make an excellent husband. He walked soberly, just
in the center of the pathway that led to the house. He
carried a most respectable brown satchel. His step was
springy, but he did not bounce.

On impulse, she leaned out over the windowsill, hoping
that he might glance up and so catch a picture of his future wife, enchantingly framed. When he failed to do so,
she shrugged, counted up to fifty in order to give John's
grandparents time to fuss over him, and then walked demurely down the front stairs. Upon seeing them all
together, she managed a little gasp of surprise and paused

on the bottom step, looking about to flee, looking exceptionally maidenly.

"Oh, there you are," said Mr. Jeremy.

"This is Katie," his wife said. John looked at Katie, gave a brief nod and waited for enlightenment. Mrs. Jeremy enlightened him. "Katie Thorne. She came into our lives out of a storm, like a little lost lamb . . ."

Katie suppressed a wince, but her future husband—for, thought Katie, that was what he was—seemed unperturbed. No doubt he was used to this kind of thing.

". . . and the dear child," his grandmother burbled on, "has been persuaded to stay with us for a few days . . ."

Persuaded! Katie cast down her eyes.

". . . and she is the greatest help around the house, John, quite indispensable . . ."

Exactly!

". . . and you will love her."

This time, John achieved a slight bow. Katie responded with an equally slight curtsey, tailored to her station in life, and then flashed her green eyes up at him to get a good look. His hair was rather flatter than it had seemed from above, and about the color of his satchel. He had a round pale face, a very everyday face, and round pale eyes, and he looked like his grandparents grown young.

Her own green eyes widened, and they held his for an intentionally long moment. Most oddly, he gave no sign of drowning and, for a moment, Katie was almost offended. No matter. Drowning would come. For the present, she was very well satisfied. He did not flop about like the Mooncalf, nor act toward his relatives like that poor Timothy Doormat. He was not a crowing rooster, like Adam, and, most important of all, he was not a married man like Eben.

"I've tidied your room for you," Katie said, smiling at him.

Mrs. Jeremy bobbed approval. "She's as neat as a pin."

"Good," said John Taggit, approving neatness. He nodded once all round, picked up his satchel, and went up the stairs.

"Well," said Mr. Jeremy, "that's his way."

Katie smiled, having a way of her own.

A week later, she was not so sure. The object of her undivided attention was perfectly polite, perfectly friendly, perfectly remote. When she came in to dust his desk, sometimes hourly, he did no more than move his papers out of her path and say thank-you. When she lingered in his doorway, round chin nestled on round shoulder, he resisted her irresistible grace.

The mirror in her small bedroom, as well as the mirror in the downstairs hall, constantly reassured her, but she turned from them sighing. She could not stay in this house forever, and, to tell the truth, she was getting unbelievably bored. Sometimes, she thought of picking up her bag and leaving by the back door, but then she told herself sternly that it was too soon. She schooled herself to tedium and quiet, and lived the life of a neat little cat waiting for a neat little mouse.

On the eighth day, in an afternoon of extravagantly golden sun, virtue was rewarded. John broke his routine and took himself to the grassplot in front of the house, where he sat down in the shade of the shade tree and drew a small book from his pocket.

Watchful at the front window, feather duster on the alert, Katie studied the terrain.

His grandparents, she knew, would be napping in their

bedroom, where they napped circumspectly every afternoon, side by side on their double bed, dozing, waking. Occasionally, she heard them talking drowsily—tranquil scraps of conversation, the very thing she had in mind for herself and John when they were ripe with years. Old people could go on like that forever, she supposed, knitting up their words like a wool scarf, ripping out the stitches, and knitting them up again. As for herself, she had better get started.

Flinging the feather duster away, she headed out the front door, tripped across the grass, and joined John Taggit under his tree. Her shadow fell on his page, and he looked up with a frown that was almost audible. Katie did not care to be frowned upon, but she sat down, spread her skirt, and swallowed her dissatisfaction. "Your grandmother thinks that you read too much," she said.

"I have to," he said. "I'm studying."

"It's bad for the eyes," said Katie, "to read in the sunlight."

"I cannot," he said, "read in the dark."

She thought he was making a joke and shot a hopeful look at him, but he was sober as an owl. Perhaps he had no sense of humor at all, like the gentleman boarder who had roared into the Thorne household one day, emerging from the far, far West (wherever that was), with coins jingling in his pocket and a wide-brimmed hat. A sweet creature he had been and almost too jovial, but never once during his stay had he understood a joke, not even those that were carefully explained to him. They had all tried, over and over, but he only fixed them with his fine eyes in passionate, and somewhat exhausting, enthusiasm. What he lacked in humor, he had more than made up in energy, and Katie's fleetness of foot was at times sternly tested. The far, far West, it seemed, bred nimble men.

126

Remembering the gentleman boarder, she looked at John Taggit now and tried again. "Would you like a cup of tea? I could bring it out to you."

He thanked her, no.

"Milk?"

"No, thank you."

"Whiskey?" said Katie despairingly.

"I don't drink." He paused. "Thank you."

Katie folded her hands in her lap and raised her eyes to a blue, unhelpful heaven. "I am very glad to hear that," she said with piety. "Once, when I was wandering on the road, I met a man who had been drinking. Heavily." Poor old James the Junkman, she sacrificed him without a thought. "He—he . . ." John did not appear to be observing the effect of fluttering eyelashes, so she transferred the flutter to her voice. "He was very—I mean, it was—Of course, I didn't let him . . ." She trembled, and looked down.

He laid aside his book at once. "Child," he said, "you must be more careful of your associates."

Child, indeed! He was all of four years older than she was, with a chin as downy as a baby chick. She bent her head even lower and said, "It's hard for a young woman alone in the world." The phrase pleased her. The hand of the young woman alone in the world escaped from her lap and strayed toward the young man. The faintest of sighs parted her lips—rose-petals, as Mrs. Jeremy might have observed with her gift for candied thoughts.

John's duty was perfectly clear. All he needed to do was to clasp the little hand that quivered toward him, draw its owner to his heart, and promise that she need never be alone again.

She looked down at the little hand. It lay there, on the grass, quite unclasped. With a faint feeling of impatience, she repeated her words—"It's hard to be alone." Even to her own favoring ears, she sounded like nothing so much as what Mr. Porter forthrightly called those damn mourning doves, which woke regularly at dawn, complaining and moaning, just outside Mama's window where the curtains were coral pink.

Katie pulled her thoughts away from Mama's curtains, which she had always admired, and moved her hand along until it encountered John's sleeve. It remained there, a feather's pressure.

"You need a husband," John said thoughtfully.

The feather firmed. Katie swayed toward him, raised her emerald eyes. "Yes?" she said, then abandoned the question mark. "Yes."

He turned his head, and their eyes met. Her fingers tightened on his sleeve. She swayed some more, a flower in the wind.

"We must find you one," said John.

The world, which had been tipping so smoothly and at just the right angle to pitch her into his arms, lurched. The rose-petal mouth dropped open, the emerald pools in which John Taggit was supposed to be floundering widened into lakes.

Failing to hear the faint sound made by the gritting of pearly teeth, John went right on. "Of course, you're young," he said. "You've probably not thought of marriage yet."

She took her hand back into her own possession and sat there in the sunlight, simmering with indignation and unusually beautiful if only someone would look at her. Either John Taggit had a total lack of self-confidence, which was unlikely, or she had no charms for him, which was unthinkable, or his head was made of solid wood, which was a genuine possibility.

128

"I *have* thought of marriage," she said at last, and added, "Often."

"Splendid."

Well, at least he approved of the idea, which was more than some mothers and sisters did. Feeling the need for refinement in her diction, she said carefully, "You believe in matrimony?"

"Oh, yes. Yes, indeed. It's an excellent thing."

Katie smiled her most joyous smile, but John was staring into space and missed it. He's pale as a candle, she thought critically, and wondered why, at his age, he was still a student. At his age, he ought to be a married man, and in this project she was fully prepared to assist him. In the meantime, all she asked was that he turn his head and gaze deep into her eyes. It is hard for a man to think of scholarly matters when he is gazing deep into the eyes of something female.

He cleared his throat, and Katie readied herself once more to hang on his words. None came; he had merely been clearing his throat. She tried again. "Some people don't believe in matrimony, you know."

He brightened at once and nodded. "Saint Paul."

"Saint Paul?"

"Not for men anyway," said John.

She thought about this very hard for a moment, and then she said, "But how can the women marry if the men don't?"

He frowned and said that it was in the Bible, and, since he seemed to be reproving her logic, she changed the subject. "Is that what you're reading now?" she asked. "The Bible?"

He glanced down at the book in his lap and said no, this was a tract, and then he added, somewhat defensively, "After all, you know, I *am* a theology student."

She had not known, and indeed she was not much wiser now, but she had a feeling that, if asked to explain theology, he would do so and at great length. In their golden years, there would be plenty of time for explanations. However, she was eager to share his interests, and she said brightly, "I was born in a convent."

He turned and stared at her. "Roman?"

Katie said, "Massachusetts," rather doubtfully. Mama's geography had never been very dependable.

"I mean, Catholic," he said. "Are you a Roman Catholic?" His face was suddenly stern, and she could tell that somehow she had displeased him.

"I mean a hospital, not a convent," she offered hastily. "The nuns were Catholics, not me. All of us came in out of a terrible storm. . . ."

"All of us?"

"Mama and me and—" She caught herself just in time, aware that the introduction of all those sisters was bound to damage the useful image of a young girl alone in the world. However, it was all right to mention Mama, who would certainly have been present at her daughter's birth. "Mama and me," said Katie, very firmly.

"I see," said John. "And your mother—?"

"She abandoned me," said Katie, absolutely inspired.

"My dear child!" All doubt abruptly left his voice. He reached impetuously for her little hand. "My dear Katie—"

Her fingers clasped his before they could get away. She breathed a "Yes?" and moved considerably closer, permitting the summer breeze to waft her gently against his shoulder. Having arrived there, she nestled. This time, although he continued to stare straight ahead, he managed to press the little hand with which his own was now so inextricably entangled.

They remained thus for a short time, while she patiently waited for him to realize that he still had one hand free. All he needed to do was to put that hand under her round chin, tilt her sweet face up to his, and seal the bright day with a kiss. After which, like Timothy Cassidy, he would say Katie-will-you-marry-me? and she would permit herself to fall tenderly, inexorably, into his eager arms. Unlike Timothy Cassidy, his relatives would be delighted.

She sighed. He sighed. He put his hand under her round chin. She lifted her face encouragingly. . . .

Nothing happened.

She waited a long moment, disbelievingly, and nothing continued to happen. Never in all her life had she met such a man for letting nothing happen. It confirmed Mama's frequently expressed opinion that it was a woman's destiny to get things moving. Accepting this, Katie said "John" in a whisper, shaping her lips over his name, offering them soft and warm and ready to become a kiss.

He moved slightly—a mere twitch, a tremor. "Katie—"

"Yes, John?"

"Nothing," he said, and to her dismay she felt him withdraw from the grip he had on her, which was rapidly turning into the grip she had on him. They could stay stuck there forever, his hand under her chin, her neck breaking, the right and necessary words unsaid.

"John?" she said again, and moved closer.

He withdrew. They might have been performing a seated minuet, and no doubt they could go on forever, advance, retreat, advance, retreat, John, Katie, John, your turn next. Here was a man in the perfect posture to offer matrimony, and all he seemed to be able to do was to breathe, and that heavily. She would never, she thought indignantly, get him at such a ripe moment again, and there was no guarantee that she could hold him in it now. Any second, Mrs. Jeremy might come popping out on the front steps, calling yoo-hoo-my-dears like a misguided cuckoo clock.

It was a moment of decision, and Katie decided.

Without pausing to consider consequences, she flung her arms around his neck. "John!" she cried, and added, by way of establishing possession, "My darling!"

It was totally the wrong thing to have said. John leaped up as if she had stuck a pin into him, and, in leaping, he leaped away. The intertwined fingers, the hand under the chin, the perilous nearness of two mouths, the encircling arms—all to no avail!

Her fourth potential mate snatched from her grasp just at the moment of victory, Katie did the only rational thing. She burst into tears.

It was as pitiful as it was effective. John, leaping away, leaped back. He hovered above her, making small desperate noises. "Katie, please . . . Katie, please, don't . . . Katie!"

Very encouraging. She looked up at him through glittering eyelashes, letting the great crystal drops spill over from her green, green eyes and course down the peach-bloom of her cheeks. She appeared to be quite helpless to check the lovely rain.

John cried out again, in protest. "Katie, you mustn't . . ."

"I c-c-can't help—" A shapely sob intervened. "I c-c-can't h-help it." Never was a hiccup so moving. She choked back another, and, gallantly, she raised one white finger to catch one last dewy teardrop.

"Katie!"

Timidly, and in a voice as tiny as a doll's, she rebuked herself. "Oh, I shouldn't have spoken, John. It was wrong of me." She paused for reassurance. None came, but the silence seemed receptive and she went on. "It's just that you—Oh, John, you are so wise and strong. And I—" It was the faintest but least inaudible of murmurs—"I am so alone." She let that sink in, and then, lying in her teeth, she added, "I need someone to look after me."

She stole a quick upward glance, and (as usual) the wretched man was staring off into space. She waited (as usual), and at last he said, morosely, "This is all my fault."

She supposed that he must mean that he was the one who should have taken the initiative, which was certainly no less than the truth. Folding her hands into her lap, she waited for him to correct his omission. Five words would do it—Katie, will you marry me?—and she suppressed the impulse to prompt.

"Yes," said John, "it *is* my fault." He then rearranged his italics and said, "It is *my* fault." He drew himself up, and, seeming to gain strength from altitude, he drew himself up a bit further. From where she sat, his feet now looked rather large and his head rather small. "Katie—"

"Yes, John?" she said breathlessly.

"Katie," he said, "I shall always treasure this moment."

How sweet, thought Katie, wishing he would get past the introduction.

"Always." He paused, thought, and began again. "I shall always treasure this moment. . . ."

You said that before, said Katie, not aloud.

". . . and I am deeply touched." He bowed his head, and there is every reason to believe that his sigh was sincere. "I am touched by your—by the depth of your feelings, my child, but the fact is—I think you should know—I am not in a position . . ."

"Are you trying to tell me," said Katie, rashly, "that you don't want to marry me?"

He looked up at the heavens, and the change in perspective seemed to encourage him. He spoke firmly. "I do not intend to marry anyone, Katie," he said, and, when she stared at him, he added, "I am entering the ministry."

Her relief was as profound as her shock. "Oh, if that's all," she exclaimed, "there's no problem, John. Lots of ministers marry. In fact," she added, rather didactically, "ministers are supposed to marry. It's not moral if they don't."

He winced and shook his head. "No, my dear, ministers often take a vow to be celibate."

"To be *what?*" said Katie.

"Celibate."

There was a silence while she tried the word over in her head (it was certainly very musical), and then she made a wild guess. "Faithful?"

He hesitated. "Uh—unmarried."

"No wives at all?"

"None."

"Never?" she said.

"Never." His voice strengthened, and then, unable to resist the human urge for that fatal one touch too many, he added, "In fact, I have forsworn women."

She sat there in the long grass, astounded and staring, and, as she stared, her astonishment turned to honest outrage. For days, she had been behaving like an angel of light in this Taggit household, practically giving them the best years of her life, and at no point had anyone given her even the faintest warning that she was wasting her time, squandering her energies, and embarked on a futile quest! A basic fairness did compel her to admit that John had a perfect right to be celibate if he wanted to be—after all, Mama, Clovelly, Octavia and Dawn were all unmarried, so they were celibate too—but that he should stand there, looking down at her from his insufferable altitude, brazenly announcing that he was forswearing women . . .

Coward! thought Katie witheringly, and jumped to her feet. This brought her directly under John's nose, her brow a thundercloud, her eyes on fire. Pinned like a butterfly on that green gaze, John turned pale, then quite pink. As he did so, he began to diminish and revert to his normal size, to become strawlike and even faintly preposterous.

He started to say something, faltered, then seemed to recollect himself. The recollection apparently did him good. His shoulders braced, his chin stabilized. When he spoke, his voice was mellow, as from a distant pulpit. "Katie," he said, "I want you to know that I shall always treasure this moment, and that I shall always—"

She turned and left him without a backward glance.

Sixteen ∾

Katie waited until the next morning to shake the dust of the Taggit household off her feet. Arising at dawn, she wrote a note to the entire family, announcing formally that she had felt the call of the open road and had returned to her life of wandering. These phrases, which were certainly beauteous, swam into her mind unsought, and, by the time she had spelled each word with anxious care (though not always successfully), she had begun to feel like an author.

Adding a really thrilling flourish on the F in Farewell, she re-read her work with respect, signed it K. Thorne, and put on her shoes. Then she took up her bag, looked once and unsentimentally around the little room, walked sedately downstairs to the kitchen, assembled a hasty breakfast, and let herself out the back door with the first rays of the morning sun and the voice of the first waking sparrow.

She had no idea where she was going now and she cared less, so she followed where her shoes took her and gave her mind over to studying her problems, of which John Taggit had been such a recent and major one.

Well, she was rid of him now, but it did seem trying that, in a world so full of men who took such a sincere interest in women, she had been fated to meet one with such odd ideas. Perhaps if John had heard about Noah before he heard about Saint Paul, things would have been different.

Katie sighed. Her needs were so simple: a man, to marry. Other women seemed to get husbands easily enough, look at Mrs. Cassidy. There was known to be a Mrs. Cornelius Porter, and there was even a Mrs. James the Junkman. Emma Swann had once achieved a husband, though, understandably, she had walked out on him.

Remembering Emma, Katie also remembered that last merry wave of her hand, so oddly like Clovelly in a person so different. It would be nice to see Emma again, pick up that interesting conversation where it had left off, find out how things were doing on the hilltop. Perhaps, by now, the store had many customers—old ladies in search of canned soup and brown sugar, old men in search of boot polish and pipe tobacco, young men in search of brides.

Instantly, she pictured the perfect young man standing before her. He would be tall and handsome (he might as well be, she figured, no sense wasting a daydream on someone short and plain) and, the moment he laid eyes on her, he would want her for his own. She would smile at him, widen her own green eyes—

She did so now, practicing on the scenery, and then she

137

blinked and widened them further, not artistically. The scenery was not only familiar, its familiarity pounced at her—a copse of trees, a meadow, a distant barn. And beyond them in plain sight, Emma's hilltop.

She had been walking half the morning in the wrong direction, and—call it Fate and not to be argued with, or call it womanly intuition, or just call it simple dumbness—here she was, exactly where she wanted to be. She decided to call it Fate.

The sign that said GROCERIES BEER was still swinging crazily; the door of the little building was still ajar. The boxes and the white bug powder were unchanged, and the potatoes had given up hope. Katie pushed open the door and walked in.

Same dark room, same smell of dust and licorice, same shelves, same dill hanging from same hook. But, this time, there was no one behind the counter.

The back door was wide open, and Katie went out through it, convinced now that Emma must have moved on. Back to Eben? north to the polar bears? south ahead of the birds? She looked around her, and then she gave a cry of alarm.

Flat out, arms spread wide, chin to the sky, and eyes closed, lay Emma Swann.

She's dead, thought Katie melodramatically, Eben's come and killed her. She then thought, no, she looked so nice and peaceful, maybe she had been struck by a thunderbolt. What did one do for a person struck by a thunderbolt?

In that moment of indecision, peaceful Emma yawned, sat up, and said "Oh, hello" in the friendliest fashion imaginable. Katie said, accusingly, "I thought you were dead."

Emma said, no, she wasn't, and reached around to pick some stray twigs off her shoulder blade. She was some ways the same as when Katie had left her, and some ways different. Her face wasn't soft wax any more, she seemed to have filled out a bit around the edges, and her eyes were no longer brown pebbles but bright as a squirrel's. "Why did you think I was dead?" she asked.

"Well, you looked dead."

"Thanks," Emma said dryly, then added, "I always lay out here. It's the nicest place I've ever been, and nobody comes. Except you."

"Eben didn't?" Katie said.

"I'm wrong," Emma acknowledged. "Somebody did come. Eben sent up a boy and a message, along with a jug of wine. Said if I didn't come down off the hill in twenty-four hours, he'd come and get me, and the wine too."

"Did he?"

Emma shook her head. "No, I sent a message back that I had a gun."

"Do you?"

"No," said Emma. "What would I want with a gun?" She then added, "Do you like wine?"

"Not much."

"That's all right, he probably put rat poison in it."

Katie, who had been looking at her very hard, said, "You sound a lot cheerfuller than when I left you."

"*You* don't," Emma said. "Things go wrong? Or are you hungry?"

"I'm hungry," Katie said, very quickly.

Emma waved vaguely toward the little store. "There's some decent biscuits now and apples and stuff. Eben's boy came in handy to bring me things, real nice of Eben, though it wasn't what he'd planned. Lots of things about me that Eben never planned." There was a gleam in the

139

bright squirrel eyes. "The bread's turned mouldy, I'm afraid, but there's cheese if you don't mind it tougher than leather."

"I'm not really hungry," Katie said.

Emma nodded. "So things *did* go wrong."

"Well, yes, I guess you could say they did." She sat herself down, put her chin on her knees, and stared at the ground—good brown dirt with green weeds and grass growing in it, full of springiness. Nobody said anything, just the two of them sitting there, and after a while Katie began to feel as if she was sitting with Dawn.

"I guess you didn't get married yet?" Emma said finally.

"No, I guess I didn't," said Katie, and then brightened. "But I got two offers."

"Did you really?" said Emma, and she even sounded like Dawn.

"No," said Katie. She felt suddenly as tired as sin, and she let herself slide full length down onto the grass and the ground, all in a heap. "I didn't get *any.*"

"You still fixed on marrying?"

Katie said yes, and, when Emma shrugged and asked why, she added, a little defensively, "It's because of Noah."

"Noah? He one of the ones that didn't make an offer?"

Katie explained about Noah, and, because she had heard the story so many times, she told it now in Dawn's exact words. It was a very good and reassuring story, and, when she had finished it, she waited for applause.

Emma, however, merely said, "You must be crazy. Who told you all this?"

"My sister. Her name's Dawn."

"Does *she* believe that everything's supposed to go two by two?"

140

Katie reluctantly said no. "Neither do my other sisters. And neither does Mama."

"Dear Lord!" said Emma sincerely. "You got a Papa too?"

"I did have, but Mama can't remember who he was."

Emma said she would like to meet Mama. "How many sisters you got?"

"Three."

"I wish I had even one," Emma said. "If I'd had a sister, maybe I'd never have got stuck with Eben."

Katie said, "Well, of course, you were unlucky. He *is* an ape, like you told me."

Emma shot her a startled look. "You met him?"

"Well, yes. You told me that he had three brothers, and I thought maybe one of them would be—There wasn't any harm—" She then said, with unnecessary loudness, "Emma, it wasn't Eben I was after. You said yourself that the second one—Adam—wasn't so bad." She waited for Emma to say something, but Emma was waiting for her. "I got along quite well with Adam, as a matter of fact, and when I told him to get out of my room, he got out."

"My," said Emma, "you have been busy." After a moment, she said, "What about Benjy and Harold?"

"Are they the peasticks?"

"You could call 'em that." Emma sounded rather pleased.

Katie sat up, stuck her legs out in front of her, and stared at her shoes. "As a matter of fact, I never really got to know them. Eben . . ."

"What about Eben?"

The merest trace of a smile curved Katie's mouth. "Eben tripped backwards over a bench."

"Tripped?" said Emma. "Backwards?"

"Well, I—" Katie walked her fingers daintily through

the grass, then looked up. The smile was now almost out of hand. "Well, to tell you the truth, I pushed him. Quite hard."

Emma gave her a look of purest affection. "You *pushed* him?"

"Yes. Quite hard. The last I saw of Eben, he was flat on his back and yelling."

"Flat on his back," Emma said contentedly. "And yelling."

With all due modesty, Katie explained that she had strong wrists. They sat for a bit longer, each thinking her separate thoughts, and then Katie said, "So that didn't work out so well."

"It worked out beautifully," Emma assured her. "I only wish I'd been there to see.—So that was your first offer, was it?" Her voice put quotes around the word. "What happened to the second one?"

Katie began, "I wasn't really lying . . ." but Emma cut her short. "Sure you were lying, Katie. Women always lie about men."

Katie sighed. "The truth is," she said slowly, "I never thought that finding a mate was going to be all this difficult."

"You mean a husband, don't you, not a mate?"

"It's the same thing."

"No, it's not," Emma said firmly. "Eben's a husband, but he's not a mate, and your father was a mate but he wasn't a husband. What you want is a husband, and it beats me why." Katie started to answer, and Emma flapped a shushing hand. "I know—Noah. I don't believe in Noah."

"He's in the Bible."

"He should stay there," said Emma ruthlessly.

142

"Then you're more like Saint Paul." Katie was thinking deeply. "And Saint Paul is more like my sisters, because he didn't believe in matrimony and neither do they. John Taggit said—"

Emma put her hands to her head. "Who's John Taggit?"

Responding to the invitation, Katie told her about John Taggit in considerable detail, and then ended on a note that was not altogether mournful. "He told me he was celibate—" (she pronounced the word respectfully) "—and he said that meant he had forsworn women. And then, he said for about the tenth time that he would treasure this moment forever, and then I walked out on him."

"Good."

"And, before him," said Katie, who was now wound up, "there was Timothy Cassidy. His mother said I was a whore, and we *all* walked out, me and all my family, I mean. And, before Timothy, there was the Mooncalf. I can't remember his name, but he really did propose. I said no." She sounded puzzled. "I don't know exactly why. I could have made him over after we got married."

"Don't you believe it," Emma said. "Men don't want to be made over. Women, neither.—Is that the lot?"

"Except James the Junkman, and you can't count him. I took his horse."

Emma was clearly entranced by this new development, and Katie explained that she had only borrowed the animal. "You see," she went on, "I thought that, if I left home, I would surely find some man who—"

"Three sisters, and no men at home?" Emma sounded skeptical, and Katie hastened to reassure her at some length. "Sounds like a paradise for brides-to-be," Emma said finally. "Why didn't you just stay there and pick 'em

143

off the trees?" She answered her own question. "Of course, if your family's against matrimony, that makes a difference. My folks couldn't see me married and out of the house quick enough. I don't exactly blame them. I'm a bramble bush." She stretched her arms up to the sky and gave half a laugh. "If I was you, Katie—which God forbid—I'd go home to my own backyard and let the bees come to the honey."

Katie frowned. "But I can't. I left a note saying that I was bringing home a mate."

"Husband."

"Husband."

Emma shrugged. "Listen, you've got three choices. You can go home and find a husband there where the pickings are rich, or you can take to the road again and look for a husband, which is hard on the feet."

"What's the third choice?" Katie said anxiously.

"Forswear marriage," Emma said blandly. "At least, for a while.—You're young, Katie. Quit hunting, and treat yourself to a year off. Have a holiday."

"But—"

"It would do you a world of good," Emma told her, sounding benevolent. "You need a real rest." She was starting to slide gently down onto the ground, taking herself out of the conversation. Fearful of losing her audience, Katie cried out, "But a whole year! What would I do for a whole year?"

"Why not go home?" Emma said. She was full length now, stretched out on a world that seemed just to fit her. "Your home sounds like a great place for forswearing matrimony," she added, and gave a drowsy laugh.

"But I left a note. I told them . . ."

There was no answer. Flat out, arms spread wide, chin to the sky, and eyes closed, lay Emma Swann.

Just like she was when I came, thought Katie. Contented as a cow in a pasture. Eben wouldn't like all that contentment, nor Adam either, nor even Benjy and Harold. Thinking about the four brothers, Katie put her chin on her knees again and thought some more. She thought about John Taggit and Timothy Cassidy, and about the Mooncalf whose name she now remembered was Arthur Bean, and then she thought about Mr. Cornelius Porter, and, last of all, about Mama and Clovelly and Dawn and Octavia.

She thought about them all, at exhausting length, and then she thought about Emma's advice. Her green eyes turned very dark, and there were two delicate lines between the brows that arched over them. She began to plait some long grasses together, made a bracelet for her wrist, threw it away, made a ring. The ring broke and turned itself back into grassblades, and then Katie threw them away too and got softly to her feet. The grass must have rustled in Emma's ears.

Without moving, Emma said, "You're leaving."

"Yes."

"I figured. You know where you're going?"

"I'm going home," Katie said, "and I'll tell them I've decided to forswear matrimony, like you said." She then added, very firmly, "But not for a whole year, Emma, that's too long. I'm going to forswear it for six months. Six months exactly."

Emma opened her eyes and gave a faint nod. "You've got a real tidy mind," she said. "You'll enjoy an Ark."

Katie nodded in return, and then, when Emma closed her eyes again, she started to walk away.

"Katie—"

She said yes, without looking back.

"I just wanted to thank you," said Emma, "for laying

145

Eben out flat on the floor. I appreciate that, I really do."

"You're welcome," said Katie, and added to her own surprise, "I enjoyed it."

"I figured," said Emma.

Seventeen ॐ

By late afternoon, Katie had lost herself twice and was still a long way from home, but she had been walking with such peculiar jubilance that she could have walked forever on any road and climbed over the edge of the world, if her shoes would hold out.

Time stretched ahead, free and clear into eternity—or at least for six months, which was nearly as good. *You're young,* Emma had told her hearteningly, just when she had been feeling older than Noah himself, four possible husbands already slipped through her fingers. Six, if you counted the peasticks.

None of them mattered any more. She was as free as Emma herself, free as a gypsy, which was something she might very well become if she was in the mood. Or she might go on the stage for six months, if she chose to, and make a fortune. Or even turn herself into a lady salesman like the Mooncalf or Mr. Hermitage, and make an even larger fortune. Surely she was cleverer and more persuasive than any of the gentlemen boarders, and so were Mama and so were all her sisters. Why was there a rule that travelling salesmen always had to be men?

Injustice corrugated her brow, but, being faced in a moment with a choice between two roads, she lost interest in philosophy. She chose the right-hand one and met no one and nothing of interest along it, until a small boy with a large dog came running up to join her and, offhandedly, invited himself to keep her company wherever she might be going. He was one of those hurtling ten-year-olds, who know everything including the exact time of day and the nearest post office, and the dog was the kind that has a noble character and no ancestry at all. Katie found them both delightful, all the more so when they steered her to a small dilapidated farmhouse and a large dilapidated lady who supplied scorched eggs in chicken fat, rolls made of baked plaster, and fresh milk to wash it all down.

"You do have nice friends," Katie said as they left, in a benediction of good wishes for the road. The boy said yes, this was because he and his dog were so nice, and he said it with such easy arrogance that she found herself wishing he was a dozen years older. He then pledged her eternal devotion and inquired if she was married. Yes, said Katie, she was, and added "To a locomotive engineer," feeling that this would please him, which of course it did. When they finally parted, they missed each other for a whole half hour.

Sustained by the episode, Katie walked on past sundown, by which time it was clear that she could not reach

Falling Grove that night and would have to sleep under a tree or in a barn, unless she could find a house as welcoming as the dilapidated lady's had been. Pursuing the intuitive logic that had brought her this far, she rejected several houses that were perfectly suitable and arbitrarily chose one that was thin, high and slit-windowed.

She went to the back door, which would surely lead to the kitchen, knocked politely, and waited. The door opened a grudging two inches, and a nose came through to point at Katie.

"Ma'am," said Katie, making a guess at the nose's gender, "I've come a long way and I'm very hungry. Do you think—?"

"No," said the owner of the nose, very sourly, and vanished. The door closed tight.

Katie shrugged, turned on the step and started to leave, then changed her mind. All that she needed was one foot in the door, a salesman's foot, and now that she had learned a salesman's first lesson (Never ask a question that can be answered by "No"), she knocked again and with more energy.

This time the whole head appeared, eyes as suspicious and narrow as the slitted windows.

"Ma'am," said Katie, "I have some pretty little things for sale " She held up her travel bag with a winning smile. "I'd like to come in for just a moment and show you . . ."

"No," said the sour head, and the hinges on the closing door almost shrieked.

Lesson number two, apparently—anything can be answered by "No." She almost turned away again, but from behind that blank door there came a hint of something irresistible. Ambrosia? Soup? Katie sniffed and raised her hand to pound once more, then stopped. Very circumspectly, she pulled her shawl up from around her shoulders and draped it over her cloud-black hair. Satisfied, she curled her hand back into a fist and set it once more to pounding at the barricade.

"Don't answer," said the sour voice from inside.

So there was someone else in there. She curled her fist tighter and hammered with vigor and zeal. The door opened so suddenly and swung so wide that she nearly fell through.

"Well, hello," said the young man cordially.

"Jo-seph," called the voice in the shadow behind him. "I told you not to answer."

"Nonsense, Auntie," Joseph said, speaking over his shoulder and studying Katie on the doorstep at the same time with an enthusiasm that penetrated the covering shawl. "You can't let a young lady faint on the threshold. It would cause a scandal." He then said, "Come in, beautiful stranger," and stepped out of her way.

Katie, appreciating the welcome, came in, pushed back the shawl and let it drop around her shoulders. She tossed her hair—only, of course, to get it out of her eyes—and then she raised those eyes to the young man named Joseph.

Bright already, he brightened even further. He was a nice-looking young man, sturdy and sandy-haired, and his own eyes were very merry and very blue. When the blue eyes met the green ones, the young man caught his breath sharply. Katie's lashes fluttered before they fell.

"Jo-seph," said the voice of Auntie, "I don't want—"

"My Aunt Hannah," Joseph explained. "She doesn't want—"

"—me to come in." Katie's voice was very small indeed, very wistful. "If I hadn't been hungry," she said, "I would never have dreamed of knocking. But," she added, from memory, "it's very hard for a young woman alone."

"*Joseph!*" It was a shriek like the door hinges.

Joseph appeared to be deaf in his nephew ears. He reached out and took Katie's hand into his large one (this had all happened somewhere before, had it not?) and led her across the room to the kitchen table, where he sat her down like a duchess. She was glad to sit, having come so far, and she kicked off her shoes, curled her toes, and gazed comfortably about her. Aunt Hannah, wherever she was, was no longer in the kitchen.

"She'll be along," said Joseph, following every turn of Katie's head, and no wonder the way her silky hair swung after it. "Don't worry."

"I can't say I was worrying exactly," Katie said, and smiled.

Joseph stared at her. "You're lovely. Would you like some soup?"

She had never known a young man with such a grip on essentials. She said thank-you demurely and yes-please greedily, and he smiled back for rather a long time before he went to the cupboard for a bowl and to the stove for a ladle. While he was thus usefully employed, Aunt Hannah suddenly appeared in the doorway, thin as a splinter, twenty feet tall, and wearing black. Katie sighed.

Without coming into the room, Aunt Hannah said, "We don't want you here."

Without turning from the stove, Joseph said, "We can't send her away, it's snowing outside."

"It's *summer*," Aunt Hannah said angrily.

"It's thundering, then."

"It's not."

"Here's your soup," said Joseph and crossed the room,

carrying the bowl carefully to keep it from slopping, and put it down in front of Katie. Then, since he was bending anyway, he dropped a light kiss on her hair. She looked up at him, down at the soup, and, ignoring the spoon, gripped the bowl with both hands. There was a thin sound from Aunt Hannah. "Is it good?" said Joseph.

"Excellent." She was pleased with him. For all the attention he was giving his aunt, she might have been cawing on the roof. If Timothy Cassidy had possessed one ounce of Joseph's independence . . . Oh, bother Timothy Cassidy!

"What would you like next?" said her attentive young man. "Cheese? biscuits? a slice of beef?"

"Beef."

"On bread?"

"Please."

"Don't go away," said Joseph, and went off once more to make pleasant small sounds of cutting and slicing and sandwiching. Aunt Hannah appeared to have been, happily, struck dumb, and Katie, without looking at her, supposed that her mouth was hanging open.

"Did anyone ever tell you," said Joseph conversationally, "that you look like a mermaid?"

"I thought mermaids had golden hair," Katie said, her eye on the beef.

"Not this one." Joseph let his voice drop just to a soft music. "This mermaid has black hair like a night princess and green eyes for men to drown in and a skin like roses and cream and a mouth like honey—Do you like your beef cut thick?"

"I do," said Katie.

The beef was delicious, and the eyes of the young man who sat opposite her were very blue. The more he watched, the bluer they became. "You talk like a poet," Katie said after a while, speaking thickly around the bread and beef.

He nodded. "That's what I am. A scribbler."

"My father was a poet," Katie said, appropriating Dawn's father without a scruple.

"Really?"

"Really." Maybe he was, for all she knew. "He wrote long poems, very beautiful, and read them to my mother."

"Odes? Epics?"

She had no notion what he was talking about, but she nodded, and he seemed very pleased. "Where's your father now?" he asked.

"Dead, in a foreign land," she told him promptly. "He abandoned my mother, and then my mother abandoned me. I was a mere infant at the time."

He made a small noise, indicating sympathy, regret and esteem. "I could make a poem about you," he said, "but you're a poem already."

"That's a pretty thing to say," she told him and handed over her empty plate.

"Joseph!" said Aunt Hannah, and, when they both turned to look, she was still there, taller and thinner and blacker than ever. "Stop that nonsense you're talking and tell that girl to leave the house."

"She's staying the night," Joseph said cheerfully.

"She is *not*."

"Oh, yes, she is. She'll have my bed, and I'll sleep down here on the floor."

"You've gone mad," his aunt said. "She'll murder us in the night—"

He nodded. "—stab us with those ocean-wave green eyes."

"She'll rob us."

"—steal all our jewels with those soft hands," Joseph went on dreamily. "And then she'll say farewell to us in that angel voice . . ."

"Joseph!"

He gave his bright laugh. "My aunt can go on like that forever," he explained to Katie, "but so can I."

Aunt Hannah jerked a stool out from against the wall and set herself upon it as upon a pedestal, a rigid black statue of displeasure. "I wash my hands of the whole matter," she said stonily.

He thanked her politely, and then he turned to tell Katie that he enjoyed sleeping on the floor and that, anyway, he would not sleep since he planned to lie awake all night, chanting her name. He then asked her what her name was.

"Katie. Katharina, really."

"Kath-a-ri-na." His voice stroked each syllable, and it sounded lovely. In spite of Aunt Hannah, she felt very happy with her latest shelter, crammed full as she was of soup and beef and bread, of flattering extravagant words and bright-blue extravagant glances.

"Katharina," he repeated, "but it doesn't rhyme with anything, and I prefer to rhyme. Some don't." He frowned. "Kate's easy enough. Late, gate? Fate? *Mate!*"

There was a knock at the door, a quick brisk knock—someone who was used to knocking on it. A flicker of satisfaction crossed Aunt Hannah's set face. "That would be Gloria," she said.

"It's her knock," Joseph agreed, and went to answer.

Katie folded her hands into her lap. Aunt Hannah did the same, but with a difference. Joseph flung the door wide, cried "Glory!" very happily, and pulled his girl into the kitchen.

She was clearly his girl, even if he hadn't taken a quick second to kiss her on her round apple cheek and pull her buxomness tight against him. She kissed him back, a warm smack like a bun from the oven, and Katie, stealing a quick look at Aunt Hannah, found that frosty countenance split for the first time by what had to be called a smile.

Katie looked at Gloria, and Gloria stared back, with eyes that were hazel and short-lashed and saucer-round. Joseph said easily, "This is Gloria. Gloria, this is Katie."

"Pleased," said Gloria, sounding doubtful.

"Delighted," said the Duchess Katharina, bending her head in graceful acknowledgement. Joseph grinned, and Katie grinned back. She, who had forsworn matrimony for the next six months, suddenly felt herself as free as a bird in the singing season. All that fuss and feathers—courting and mating and sitting about on nests—was no problem of hers. She tipped her head at Gloria, and then she tipped her green eyes at Joseph.

"Mind your manners, Joseph!" Aunt Hannah shouted. "You're keeping Gloria waiting!"

He turned at once to Gloria, and she put her broad hand into his. "You promised we'd go out tonight," she said, "but, if you don't want to—"

"I want to," said Joseph, and the soughing sound in the kitchen was Aunt Hannah breathing triumph. He dropped Gloria's trusting hand and went over to Katie.

He stood there, looking down at her, and she looked up at him. For quite a long space of time (thirty seconds, two millenniums, thereabouts) they stared at each other. Without speaking, he told her that she was the most beautiful thing that had ever crossed his path. Elaine the fair, Elaine the lovable, his eyes said, and Helen of Troy all gold, and Iseult, and Miranda on Prospero's island, and, although

155

she wouldn't have understood the names if he had spoken them aloud, she understood very well what he was telling her.

And so she looked back at him, and with her own eyes she told him that she found him entrancing and charming, and that his words made her feel like a rose in a valley and a lily on a green stalk.

At last, he took her hand up into both of his. "You'll be here when I get back?" he said, very softly.

"No," she said, even softer. "I'm going home."

"I thought you didn't have a home," he said, and she said instantly, "Oh, but I do!"

"That's what I thought," said Joseph.

Katie smiled, and he smiled back. Their eyes pledged that they would remember each other forever, or at least as far as the next bend in the road, and their smiles said that they had enjoyed every minute of their short encounter.

Then he let her hand drop, and he said goodnight. He picked Gloria up by her round white elbow and steered her out the door. You could see by the back of her head that everything was all right for her again, and you could see by the easiness of his shoulders that everything was all right for him too, and maybe even better than usual.

Behind them, Aunt Hannah said "Well!" and she managed to sound both relieved and affronted.

Katie picked up her travel bag. Then she tossed her shawl around her shoulders and went to the doorway to look out into the night. It was all dark velvet and a few stars, and rather welcoming. She could sleep in a shed or under a tree if she had to, and she was full of good food and of some delightful (if temporary) memories.

She turned on the doorstep to say "Farewell" to Aunt Hannah and to sweep her a regal curtsey. Then she went down the back steps she had come up such a short time earlier, and the smile that she had given to Joseph came back again to tilt the corners of her mouth.

She had, she thought, enjoyed herself thoroughly. Indeed, one forgot how delightful men were, when one was not trying to marry them.

Eighteen ⁓

Mr. Porter was becoming increasingly alarmed. Not only had there been no word from Katie, but Mama, formerly so swooning and apprehensive, was now behaving like a careless cat, who, having misplaced one of her kittens, had resigned motherhood.

Her daughters were used to this sort of thing; Mr. Porter was not, and he fretted. He felt he should do something, but his own position was delicate, and he was not sure what the something ought to be. He really could not ask his wife's advice, although it would probably be very good, and he certainly could not call upon the Law. A discreet inquiry had led no further than a junkman who claimed to have seen Katie on the road, heading toward the great world, and who had remarked with relish that, by now, she had probably been sold to Chinese pirates. Mr. Porter was by nature a steady man who did not believe in Chinese pirates, but he had begun to sleep rather poorly.

"It's been too long," he told Mama, "and she's very young."

Mama remained calm. "Cornelius dear, you said yourself that if anything happened to Katie, we would certainly be notified. Those were your very words."

"It's an idiotic statement," Cornelius said edgily, "and I did not make it. It was one of those idiot boarders of yours, the skinny one."

"Slender."

"Skinny."

"Slender. With beautiful eyes." She looked up at him, standing there and knitting his brows so pathetically, and added tenderly, "Don't fret. Katie's very intelligent. Just like her dear father."

"I thought you didn't know who her fa——" He caught himself, though not in time. Clovelly, who had been following the dialogue alertly, stated that Mama would never have selected a father for Katie who was not intelligent. "You have no idea how farsighted Mama is. She's like Octavia, she can foretell the future."

"Then why doesn't she foretell it?" Cornelius demanded, and, seeing Octavia wander by in a quince-colored dressing gown, he appealed to her. "When will Katie be back, Octavia?"

"Maybe months, maybe years." Octavia's mind was on other things, and she vanished like a cloud.

Cornelius suppressed a howl of rage, and Mama said reflectively, "If Katie stays away for months or years and *then* comes home . . ."

159

"With a husband," said Clovelly.

"Hush, dear!"

"I'm only speaking for Dawn."

"You don't mean to say that Dawn wants a husband too?"

"No, darling, of course not," Clovelly said patiently. "But she's quite willing for Katie to have one, I think. After all, it was Dawn who started the whole thing."

Mama agreed, "That wretched Noah," and then she asked Cornelius if he had a headache. He said he certainly did, and added rather loudly that she had not yet finished her sentence about what would happen if Katie stayed away for a long time and then came back.

Mama said she would get him some peppermint oil and started after it, but he caught her by the shoulders and turned her around. "My love!" he said imploringly.

She laid her cheek against his lapel and curved her arm around his neck. "Very well. I only started to say that, if Katie stayed away for a long time, she might come back and find us all gone and not know where to look for us." Cornelius stiffened, and she patted him down. "But it's all right," she went on. "I've just realized that we could leave a message with you."

He said, loud and clear, "You are *not* going to go away!"

"Well, some day, I suppose . . ."

"You mustn't," he said, trying not to yell. "You don't have enough sense to look after yourselves, any of you. You aren't practical, you'll get into all kinds of trouble. Confound it, I'm in charge of your affairs, and I'm not going to let you . . ."

"Dear Cornelius."

He put both arms around her and, holding her tight, he

looked into his own future. It is all true, said his heart, some day they will move away and leave you. Some day, when you're an old man, sitting in an old bank, Mama and her daughters will be somewhere else, all of them, penniless, improvident, homeless, and beautiful. And all of them, he thought glumly, having a damn good time. Dear Lord, how soft she was!

With his chin resting on her hair, which smelled of roses and violets and verbenas, of all the flowers that never tantalized him when they grew in his wife's garden, Mr. Porter closed his eyes and dictated a small prayer, scarcely more than a memorandum, instructing the Lord God, forthwith, to take action and return him to his former posture of perfect contentment. He disliked asking personal favors, especially from Someone Who was certain to be fully occupied, but he issued this small request hopefully, a sort of bank draft on his heavenly account.

The fragrance of Mama's hair drifted around his head like a halo. Breathing deep of Elysian fields and (not quite the same thing) of Heaven, Mr. Porter very slowly opened his eyes.

Katie was standing in the doorway.

Mama, feeling an earthquake tremor in the strong arms that she was enjoying so much, turned her head. "There!" she said triumphantly. "What did I tell you? Exactly like her father!"

"Welcome home," said Clovelly and went to give Katie a tight hug, then held her off at arm's length. "You look splendid, love."

This was certainly true. Katie had a sort of incandescent glow, her eyes immoderately green, her skin dusted with gold and rose, with sun and wind. Mama jumped to the logical conclusion and cried out in dismay, "Where is he?"

"Where is who?" said Katie, all innocence.

"Your husband, of course, child."

Katie shook her head.

"You didn't find one?" said Cornelius, not certain whether to approve or disapprove.

Katie shook her head again.

"How splendid," Mama said warmly, adding as Octavia once more appeared in the doorway. "Here's Katie back home, my love, and she's not going to get married after all."

"Oh, yes, I am," Katie said indignantly. "I had hundreds of proposals." A flicker in Clovelly's eye caught the flicker in her own, and she scaled down her estimate. "Dozens, anyway. But I rejected them all."

"Why?" said Mr. Porter, who was, after all, a banker.

She was pleased to be asked. "Because," she said elegantly, "I have decided to forswear marriage . . ."

Mama's glad cry was interrupted by Dawn, who had made a quiet entrance through the window. "Katie, you're home! We missed you." She then added, "I'm pleased to hear that you're forswearing marriage. It's very becoming to you."

"I missed you too," Katie said, "but you've got it all wrong. I'm not forswearing marriage forever. I'm just forswearing it for the next six months."

"Why?" said Mr. Porter.

Katie turned on him. She had expected a far more rewarding reaction to her grand announcement, and it was extremely irritating to have Mr. Porter saying *why* all the time. She said "Because!" sharply, and felt very ill-used.

"That's not an answer," said Mr. Porter, bent on self-destruction.

Mama said, "Oh, Cornelius, dear, of course it is."

162

"You're taking her side," Cornelius said.

"I am not," Mama said. "Well, of course, I am. She's my child."

"You mean, you *want* her to get married? You never used to!" Like Katie, he was beginning to feel very ill-used, and it seemed to him that the Lord God was not paying the proper attention. He had asked for peace of mind, and all he was getting was confusion.

"Cornelius!" Mama stared at him in amazement. "How can you? You know very well that I don't want Katie to marry."

"Now you're taking *his* side," Katie cried out.

"My love—"

"Mama—"

"My dear girl—"

"Katie!"

Katie gave vent to an absolutely unmodulated shriek, and (not for the first time) she spun on her heel and ran out of the room. Not for the first time, her hair streamed behind her like a stormcloud.

They heard her bedroom door slam. "Now see what you've done," said Mama, most unjustly, to her dear Cornelius.

"My dear girl—"

She leaned suddenly into his arms and said, "Oh, that wretched Noah!" There was nothing Cornelius could do by way of comfort, except to stand there patting her soft round shoulder. Still, a man could be worse employed.

Upstairs, Katie threw herself onto her bed, bounced twice, furiously, then made an instantaneous recovery from her tantrum. She lay briefly with her nose buried in the pillow before she rolled over, crossed her arms under her head and stared up at the ceiling.

The crack in the plaster, making its haphazard way from the near corner to the far corner, was as familiar as the palm of her hand and long like its lifeline. Her gaze travelled leisurely downwards to the high window, half eclipsed by a thrusting green vine. The white curtains fluttered in the small breeze, and she could see her own large stitches galloping at the hem, testimony to the Mooncalf's midnight wooing.

Remembering the occasion with some exasperation, she drummed her heels on the counterpane, then relaxed. A poor limp creature, the Mooncalf, but, after all, it was a long time ago and she had learned a lot about men since that one. In fact, at this distance, she could even feel a mild affection for him—sweet, in his way, though not as sweet as Timothy Cassidy. She sighed fleetingly, for, if Timothy had not been so infinitely mothered, Timothy would have suited very nicely.

"It was not to be," said Katie aloud, addressing the crack in the ceiling with a most refined resignation. She then changed this to "It was not so to be," which had more style, and returned to browsing through her love life. This brought her to the Swann brothers, all of whom she had knocked out of her future with that one powerful shove. Unwomanly, she supposed, and made a graceful gesture of her hand dismissing the whole family: Eben, who was an ape; Adam, who might have been manageable, and Benjy and Harold, who were peasticks and therefore not that much better than mooncalves. As for John Taggit, he had been handsome enough and appropriate, but, alas, he was not for marrying.

She came next to Joseph, who was in chronological order, and, thinking of him, she gave the ceiling a smile that would have driven him mad or to poetry. Sweet-tongued, blue-eyed Joseph, who belonged to Gloria and Aunt Hannah forever and to Katie for just as long as she chose to let him roam around in her head. He would melt soon, she knew, like sugar on the tongue, and perhaps it was this ephemeral quality that made him so delightful. This, and the fact that she had not needed to consider him as a mate. *Husband,* she corrected herself, remembering Emma.

The thought gave her, as she would have liked to phrase it, pause. Was matrimony then to be a spoiler of delight, or—to put it more simply—would a husband take the fun out of everything? Mama, Clovelly, Dawn and Octavia would say yes, and so would Emma.

Katie bit her lip.

Mr. Porter would dodge the question. She scowled.

And Noah? She smiled.

Noah would give her his blessing. Noah's Ark was her ark—two by two, paw in paw, hand in hand, arm in arm, and heart in heart. She could picture all the wives and the husbands and the animals walking together, and with them she could picture herself. Her hair would be bound back demurely, her face would glow with the most Biblical happiness, and—most important—her hand would be safely clasped in the hand of the man who walked beside her.

Now, lying on her bed, holding her breath, she could see it all so clearly that she could almost see the man too. Almost. At the last moment, he escaped.

She let her breath go and shrugged lightly. Never mind. It was all written for her in the stars, and Noah could be trusted to look after the details. In the meantime, the world was full of men, the town was full of men, the house was full of men, and she had six months ahead in

which she could study them all without the slightest
twinge of duty.

The prospect was as delightful as it was soothing, and
the corners of Katie's mouth, commas of earnest thought,
began to turn upward.

Downstairs, "Oughtn't someone to go to the child?"
Mama said.

"Whatever for?" said Clovelly.

"To comfort her," said Mama.

"For not having a husband?" said Octavia.

"Or for wanting one?" said Dawn.

Nineteen ❧

That was the month that it rained gentlemen boarders.

Fine specimens they were too, every size and shape—
some towering, some very scant; some thin as tacks, some
spherical as barrels; handsome as pigeons, plain as shovels,
cheerful as crickets, and sharp as lemons. There were hust-
lers, languishers, pouncers; there were the venerable and
the young, the ripe and the budding. They arrived at the
front door with satchels, valises, gladstone bags, cardboard
boxes, and, in one instance, a steamer trunk which stuck
sideways on the narrow stairs.

Mama and her daughters floated gently on the tide. If
meals were scant, the boarders could invent their own. If
beds were in short supply, they could sleep on the floor. If

space ran out altogether, they could move on to Falling Grove to droop under an alien rooftree. It was such an exceptional time that two firm offers were made to buy the Thorne house, and the bidders were astonished to be so instantly rejected, not knowing that the town's leading banker had hurriedly advised himself that one should never sell on a bulging market.

On the surface of this prosperity, Katie drifted like a bubble, no more tantalizing than a ripe peach just beyond grasp, no more elusive than the gold at the end of the rainbow. Enjoying herself immoderately, she bloomed and talked no more of Arks or husbands. Mama, presuming that the black lamb had returned to the fold, also presumed that Nature would take her natural course.

However, the passage of time, as well as the despondency of some most appropriate young men whose eyes had lit up expectantly at the sight of Katie, convinced Mama that Nature was not always to be trusted. Reluctantly, she perceived that she had a mother's duty, and, when the occasion and Katie came together, she seized upon them both.

It was in the morning. Mama seldom vacated her bed until noon, and it was a bed that was as plump and soft and welcoming as Mama herself, with the additional advantage of being littered with bright cushions, pretty gowns, very small children, random portable pets, flowers in and out of season, and bits of toast.

"Darling," said Mama to Katie, "do come in."

"I am in," said Katie, and sat down on the bed.

"Mind the teacup, then."

Katie minded the teacup by drinking the cold tea in it, well-sweetened and bracing. She then punched a hollow into the nearest cushion—rose velour with a gold tassel— put the cup into the nest she had created, and pulled her feet up onto the mauve counterpane. After a moment, she kicked off her shoes.

Mama, who always found silence very hard to endure, waited briefly and then commenced. "Katie, my darling," she said, "I think it is high time for us to have a little talk." She paused. "About men."

"Oh, *yes,*" said Katie enthusiastically.

With infinite delicacy, Mama gazed at the ceiling. "There are certain facts of life. . . ."

"I know them," said Katie.

The gaze came down, and Mama said crossly, "Well, I should hope so," then she reverted to her earlier elegance and announced that she was only thinking of her dear daughter's happiness.

Katie smiled a smile so secret and so satisfied that it could not fail to reassure. Mama beamed, Katie beamed back, and for a moment the room was awash with sentiment. Then, "Mama," said Katie, sitting up straight, "I want to ask you a question."

"Anything, my love," said Mama, leaning forward eagerly.

"Would it upset you," Katie said, "if I got married in a church?"

Mama sank backwards, and the pillows sank behind her. From the depths of all that softness came a heartrending gasp of incredulity, despair, and outraged motherhood. "Katie!"

"It *would* upset you," Katie said regretfully.

Mama struggled out. "I thought you had given up the whole idea of getting married. You told me you had forsworn it—your very words!"

"I told you I had forsworn it for six months, that's what I told you." Katie jumped off the bed and started to put on her shoes, then she said generously, "But if you don't want me to get married in a church, I won't do it. Just to please you, Mama."

"It's not your getting married in church that I object to . . ."

"Darling Mama!" Katie spun about and engulfed her mother in an abounding hug. "Then you *don't* mind."

Mama paused long enough to hug her back, because hugging back was a matter of principle with her, but then she shook loose and became stern. "Katie, you're just trying to confuse me. You know very well that I'm not talking about churches." Her tone changed, a wheedling angel's. "You are so headstrong, Katie. Why does my little girl want to tie herself down?"

"I don't want to tie myself down. I want to get married."

"It's the same thing." Mama flapped a weary hand. "No, don't tell me about that Noah of yours—I wish I'd never heard of the man." Her pretty fingers, fluttering about in mid-air, attracted her attention and put her in mind of Cornelius, who, had he been here, would have captured them. Cornelius, she thought, would know at once what to do with this erring child, who was too much for her poor old mother. She would lean on him. He would be wise and comforting and very . . .

Mama smiled tenderly at Katie, and Katie smiled back. The thoughts passing through her mother's head at that moment were so clearly not all that maternal.

The tide of gentlemen boarders receded, as tides and gentlemen will, and Mama, who had been hoping that sheer numbers would do for Katie's stubbornness what nothing else seemed to, remembered her decision to consult with Cornelius—that is, to make him responsible. "Dearest," she said to him one evening, when they were sitting about and holding hands, "you must have a talk with Katie."

"No, my love," said Cornelius firmly.

"Yes, dearest," said Mama.

"But I have nothing to say to her," Cornelius said, foolishly leaving the door of his argument ajar.

Mama assured him that he was a man who always said the right thing when the time came, and all he need do was to make the time come. Then she caught sight of Katie outside the window (how providential!) and called her in. "Now!" she directed Cornelius and vanished from the room, light and conscienceless as a swansdown puff and trailing over her shoulder the remark that "Mr. Porter wants to talk to you, Katie, I must run along."

Katie, who was extremely fond of Mr. Porter, came in and sat down on the sofa. He gazed at her uncomfortably. In his turn, he was extremely fond of Katie, and if the child wanted to marry, why not? Other people did. He himself believed in the institution of marriage, just as he believed in all institutions: the banks, the Weather Bureau, the Republican Party, and his wife. His heart's own love, however, did not believe in marriage, and it was plain that Katie's wilfulness was making his beloved wretched. The thing to do, Cornelius reasoned, was to find some compromise between the two of them, and the thought was reassuring. He fancied himself as something of an expert in this sort of arbitration: mortgagor, mortgagee; vendor, vendee; legator, legatee. The euphony began to run away with him, and he cleared his throat. "My dear child—"

She eyed him sweetly. "You sound just like John."

"John?"

"John Taggit."

"Who," said Mr. Porter, groping, "is John Taggit?"

"A man I stayed with while I was away," said Katie.

Mr. Porter's heart leaped. Along with holy matrimony, he also believed in convention, propriety, decorum, and the purity of womanhood, but the possibility that Katie had at last seen the light and taken another course made his hopes soar. It would solve so many problems and give so much happiness to her dear family who were so rightly concerned. . . .

"A man you stayed with!" said Mr. Porter, most hospitably (and he a pillar of the Episcopal Church). "Well, well. Taggit, eh? I knew some Taggits once, distant kin of my mother, I believe. Though the name may have been Leggett, in fact, it was. Fine people." He looked at her anxiously, wanting only her well-being. "A nice fellow, your John Taggit, I'm sure. Eh?"

Katie crossed her feet at the ankles, which should have warned him, and cast down her eyes. "He was not *my* John Taggit," she said. "He was living with his grandparents, and he was studying for the Church."

"The Church!" said the shocked vestryman.

"He had forsworn women," Katie said, managing to make three syllables out of *forsworn* and endowing the word with considerable significance.

"My poor child!"

"He kept saying *that,* too," Katie said, not complaining, just making an observation. "And I could see," she went on, "that you can't very well marry if you've forsworn women. It didn't matter, really, he was quite dull."

There was a long and very fraught silence.

"Katie—"

"Yes, Mr. Porter?"

The voice of the pillar of Falling Grove society was somewhat desperate. "Katie, do you really feel that you must—" He paused. "Marry?"

"Yes, Mr. Porter. I must." She crossed her hands at the wrists and set them in her lap, as tidy as her slippered feet upon the carpet. She looked as if she was made of dimity and lace, and Mr. Porter, quite correctly, felt that he was getting nowhere. He said, "But—" which was a singularly unfruitful syllable.

"I am content to wait," said Katie. She then added, "Are you opposed to marriage, Mr. Porter?"

"Yes! No, no, of course not! What I mean is—" He struggled wildly to extricate himself. "Of course, I am not opposed to marriage, Katie. Marriage is an admirable institution, the oldest and most binding of contracts. My dear child—" He paused. Katie was looking up at him with a lovely fervor, and her green eyes were aglow with innocence and trust.

Mr. Porter got to his feet. He crossed to her, and, lifting her slender white hands, he pressed them within his own. "There, there," he said, "don't worry your pretty little head. Mr. Right will come along."

She did not take those green eyes off him, but she did uncross her feet. "My marriage will have your blessing then?" she asked, in a voice that was as soft and demure as a butterfly lighting on a flower.

"My dear child," Mr. Porter assured her, "of course it will."

She took her hands away from him and jumped to her feet. "Oh, thank you, Mr. Porter," she cried prettily, added, "I'll go tell Mama at once," and, before he could stop her, she was gone.

"Dear Lord!" said Cornelius, not piously. He stood there, staring helplessly into space, and already he could hear the voice of his beloved saying, "Cornelius, how *could* you?"

Twenty ∿

In the front room, the clock on the mantelpiece was just striking
thirteen. On the front steps, the four sisters, clustered as
artlessly as flowers in a bouquet, sat and listened to its
slow, dishonest report. Their heads were tipped at iden-
tical angles, their half-shut eyelids hid their varicolored
eyes, their red moist lips were sweetly parted. One, two,
three, four, five, six, seven, eight, nine . . .

"Ten," said Katie.

Dawn nodded. "Eleven."

Octavia, with a playing card poised in her hand, said,
"Twelve."

"And thirteen." Clovelly finished the chime. "I must fix
that clock some day."

"Never," Octavia said, loyal to mysteries. She glanced
down at the card in her hand, said "Ah!" dramatically, and

spun it toward Katie. "There, Katie, a knave for your heart. Tall, dark, and a joy to the eyes, coming to you right out of nowhere."

Katie reached out too late, and the flying card fell to the grass between them where it lay, face up, the haughty profile turned aside. She leaned over to stare at it and to make a mild complaint. "But he's golden-haired, Octavia, not dark."

"All the knave-cards have golden hair," Octavia told her. "But this one came with the seven of Spades, and so," she said firmly, "this one is dark.—Wait, I'll find you the seven of Hearts." She ran through the cards, making them dance in her hands, and then held one out. "Here it is."

Dawn said, "Octavia, you shouldn't cheat. It doesn't work if you cheat."

"I know." Octavia sighed. "Give them back, Katie. Dawn's right."

Katie shrugged and flipped them over. The stubborn knave fell once more to the grass—this time, face down. "Oh, bother him," Katie said lightly. "Let him go."

It was at this exact moment that the white cat came streaking toward them, so white, so sudden and vivid, that it might have been a shaft of sunlight. It hurled itself straight into Katie's arms and clung there, long-furred and plume-tailed. She gave a startled "Oh" but held on tightly, as one must when one has been chosen, and the cat stared wildly up into her face with eyes as green as her own.

There was a flutter among the sisters as if a quick breeze had touched their petals. She looked up and saw a tall young man standing in front of her, a most agreeable-looking young man, with a dark, lively face, and a lock of hair that fell over his forehead. She opened her mouth to speak, but the cat dug dagger claws into her shoulder, and she yelped instead. The young man leaped to her rescue, and the cat swore. "Let go!" said the young man severely.

"I can't!" Katie said, rather indignantly since she was the injured party.

"I don't mean you—I mean the cat." He reached out and grasped the dazzling white bundle of flailing paws, laid-back furious ears and switching tail. The cat, promptly and resourcefully, went limp and permitted itself to be lifted off Katie's shoulder as if it were a bur.

"Are you all right?"

"I'm scratched to ribbons, if that's what you mean," Katie said crossly, and she rubbed her shoulder.

He said he was sorry, and he sounded so really sorry that she dismissed her wounds and glanced up at him again, through those infinitely long lashes in which so many gentlemen boarders had tangled themselves. It was her intention to forgive him with her nicest smile, but he was looking straight at her, and, this time, their eyes rather inevitably met. His were as brown as velvet, very daring, very alive.

Katie caught her breath, and, without any warning at all, the dagger of love went straight into her heart.

The silence was long. The spinning of the earth was strange. She must have swayed a little, because he reached out to steady her. His hand was very light, but the touch of it almost burned her, and she could not fathom what was making her so giddy. "Are you sure you're all right?" he said, and she could only nod.

It was Clovelly who broke the silence, gazing at him with her chrysanthemum eyes and asking, "Is that cat yours?"

"In a way she's mine," he said.

"What scared her?"

"A yellow dog. With a long tail."

"That's the Crabbs' dog," said Dawn, recognizing the description.

"Crabb is a fit name." He turned to Dawn, and she gave him a briar-bush look, rather suspicious. "What do you mean," Dawn said, "she's your cat *in a way*. Did you steal her?"

"No. She followed me from a farm outside Falling Grove. Because I fed her, I suppose."

It was Octavia who said, "Well, she hasn't followed you very far."

"Well, I didn't feed her very much."

Octavia laughed, her wide summer eyes looking exceptionally blue. "What were you doing at a farm outside Falling Grove?"

"Looking for work."

"Did you find it?"

He shook his head. "But there's other towns."

Katie cried out "Oh, no!" before she could stop herself, and they all turned to look at her. She put her hands to her cheeks and was silent, hoping that they would only think she was giddy from the sun, or weak from hunger, or unstrung by the fierce claws of the white cat.

Clovelly's gaze wandered back to the young man. "What kind of work can you do?"

"Anything." He glanced around. "Clean your yard?"

"Done," said Clovelly briskly. After all, she was the eldest.

Katie's cockleshell heart gave a lurch of joy. Without allowing herself any time to think, she said, "What's your name?"

"Bartholomew. Bartholomew Morgan."

177

Katie Morgan, she thought instantly. Katharina Morgan, Bartholomew's wife. Oh, she was glad now that she had spurned the Mooncalf, glad that Mrs. Cassidy's son had been so fainthearted, that the Swann brothers were boors, that John Taggit slept safe in the arms of his church, and that Joseph already belonged to Gloria. Without a tremor, she cast aside forever her vow to forswear matrimony for six months. She had been a child when she made it, a mere girl, unlearned in the ways of the heart. She was a woman now.

This thought may have accounted for the fact that she had lost her voice again. The silence around her was enormous, but no one seemed aware of it, and, after all, her sisters could not possibly know that Katie had found her mate.

She corrected herself—Katie had found her husband. The thought was so strengthening that she reached out her hand and placed it softly on the cat's soft fur. This brought her head just on a level with Bartholomew's shoulder, and for a moment she was hard put not to lay it there and stay so forever. It was a pleasurable and unique sensation, and only the sound of Octavia's voice roused her from it.

"That's Katie under your chin," Octavia was saying with her best social manner. Katie backed off hastily, and Octavia went on. "And that's Dawn. And Clovelly. And I'm Octavia."

He gave a slight bow to each, and so apparently did the white cat, although this may have been a trick of the sunlight.

"If you're out of work," Octavia added, "you're probably hungry," and, when he nodded, she gave him a divine smile. "Well, there's sure to be something for you to eat, and something for your cat too. If you—"

"I'll—I'll—" Katie pulled herself together. "I'll show him the kitchen, Octavia. You're busy."

Octavia said, "Thank you, dear," and fanned herself, very busily, with her pack of cards. Without being asked, Bartholomew took Katie's hand into his free one. She could feel her face turning as pale as a lily or as vivid as a sunset, and she made a tremendous effort to look perfectly calm. The three of them—Bartholomew and Katie and their white cat—moved away across the lawn.

Behind them, there rose a gentle murmur, bees at a honey hive, doves at a cote. Confident that she had successfully concealed all her emotions, Katie did not even look back but walked away alongside her Bartholomew, clutching her newfound happiness to her newfound heart.

"Mama," said Clovelly, "Katie's in love."

"Madly," said Dawn and Octavia, speaking as one.

Mama was inside what was known formally as the linen closet. It was true that it housed linen, but it also housed string, handwritten poems (whose hand?), Clovelly's surplus kindling, some garlands of paper flowers, and a gross of mousetraps, which had been the gift of an impulsive admirer travelling in Utensils & Sundries and which were far too efficient ever to be used.

"You're all talking at once," Mama complained, backing out in a very rounded manner and bringing with her what appeared to be an ancestral tapestry.

"Katie," Clovelly repeated, "is in love."

Mama clasped the tapestry to her heart. "At last! Which one is it?"

"He's new. She's feeding him in the kitchen, and then he's promised to clean up the yard. And then I suppose he'll stay around for a bit."

"And she *loves* him?"

"Instantly. She was quite dizzy for a moment, but, of course, it's never happened to her before."

Mama glowed sentimentally. "There's nothing like the first time," she agreed, "and I'm sure he's charming." She shook out her tapestry, stared at it, wondered what she wanted it for, then added, "Thank goodness! She'll enjoy it all so much, and it will get those ridiculous ideas out of her head."

Dawn sighed. "I hope so, Mama. But she's very stubborn."

"But, my darling," Mama said, "there's no alternative." She then looked sharply at each daughter in turn, and her brow clouded. "You can't mean that he wants to *marry* her?"

"Oh, I hardly think so," said Clovelly. "He's not what one would call the marrying kind." She turned to her sisters for confirmation. "Dawn?"

"Well—no."

"Octavia?"

"Hardly."

"Then," Mama announced, instantly unclouded, "there's nothing to worry about." She smiled at them contentedly and wandered off, making maternal noises and waving the tapestry like a triumphal banner.

Dawn lifted her long brown hands in a vague gesture, then let them fall. "I hope Mama's right," she said.

Clovelly, as comforting sister, said, "She usually is, dear."

"Well, at least the playing cards were right," Octavia said, a trifle smugly. "He's very soft-spoken, Bartholomew is, but if ever I saw a Knave of Hearts . . ."

They left it there.

Twenty-one ᕦ

The white cat was the first to feel the benefits of first love. There was thick cream in the blue saucer that Katie put down on the kitchen floor, and whatever tension may have existed between the two green-eyed creatures dissolved at once.

Cream for cats was easy, but Bartholomew was not a cat, although he sat at the table as relaxed as one, his long legs crossed and his brown velvet eyes as bold as any marauder at a mousehole. Katie gave him bread and butter, a dish of something concocted by Octavia from wild plums, salt in a majestic pewter shaker, sugar in a glass jar, a red apple, a dish of yellow custard, and a honeycomb on a green plate.

He ate intently, while Katie stood by the table and watched him, her hands clasped loosely in front of her, her eyes fixed on the top of his head. She already thought of him as hers, and it was now plain why all those young men had crossed her path and gone their separate ways. Noah, the heavens, the stars, and Octavia's Knave of Hearts had ordained Bartholomew.

"Why don't you sit down?" said the object of all this supernatural attention.

She did so. He nodded and reached for the butter. After a while, he said, "I was starving," and a little later, "You're an angel.—Are you all sisters?"

Katie said yes.

"You don't look alike," he observed, "except that you're all beautiful."

She murmured agreement, having no reason to doubt his judgment. When the bottom of the custard dish was finally revealed, the white cat heard the scraping spoon and jumped onto Bartholomew's knee. He put the dish down on the floor for it to lick the edges, then he drank from the milk pitcher, emptying it with his head thrown back. When he put the pitcher down, he continued to stare at the ceiling. "This is a nice house," he said finally.

Katie agreed. They would live here together, husband and wife. So must Noah and his wife have regarded the Ark. "It's a bit draughty in winter," she said, "but Clovelly has stuffed most of the chinks with rags and paper."

"Which is Clovelly? I've got them mixed."

"The—" She found herself hesitating. "The tall one." That was odd, because the way to describe Clovelly should have been as the one with the golden eyes.

"And Octavia?"

"Blue eyes," Katie said briefly.

"Then Dawn is the third one. You'd have to look at her twice, I think, to know what color *her* eyes are. They're like a gypsy's."

"My eyes," said Katie recklessly, "are green."

"I noticed," said Bartholomew. He had just discovered the honeycomb and was letting the white cat share it with him, somewhat stickily.

Katie looked at the two of them, and then she said, "When did you ever meet a gypsy—Bartholomew?" It was the first time she had used his name.

"On the road—Katie."

She would have liked to hear him say Katharina, but Katie was joy enough. "Near Falling Grove?" she asked, just so he would go on talking.

He laughed, and the white cat jumped from his knee and went to sit under the table and to meditate on honey and its paws. "A gypsy would die in Falling Grove," Bartholomew said. "To tell you the truth, I only met one gypsy in my life, and he sold me a lucky charm. Which," he added, "I lost."

She would give him a new one. On his wedding day. "Did you mind?" she said.

"Losing the charm? No, I travel light."

She said quickly, "That's what *I* like to do," since two could surely travel as light as one. "You know, I've just come back from a very long journey. All by myself." She studied him from out of the corner of her eye, and then said, very sweetly, "But it's nicer, of course, to be with someone you like to be with. On a journey, I mean."

He pushed the table away from him and got to his feet. "Shall I do the yard now? I made a promise to that sister of yours with the gold eyes."

He already knew they were gold, and she need not have been so grudging. "Clovelly," she said.

He agreed. "Clovelly."

"*My* proper name is Katharina." She raised the fringe of her eyelashes.

"Katharina." He nodded. "Green eyes."

He looked straight into them, and Katie, who was so accustomed to providing shipwreck for others, drew a shipwrecked breath. For one heady moment, she believed he was about to sweep her into his arms and ask her to marry him, but a sounder portion of her brain warned her this was too optimistic. She estimated it might take as much as a week. . . .

"So there you are!" cried Mama.

They turned to find her in the doorway, looking authentically ravishing and just mature enough to be the mother of four beautifully ripe daughters. One could see that Bartholomew was plainly pleased and that Mama was absolutely delighted. Their eyes rested on each other most amicably.

"This," said Katie proudly, "is Bartholomew Morgan."

"I know." Mama gave to Bartholomew the look she had been giving men from the cradle, a matter of tilting the head down and the corners of the eyes and mouth up. It could only be done by instinct, as she and her daughters did it, and not by design as other less gifted females might, and it had been the cause of some acrimonious remarks in several Falling Grove households.

"He's going to clean up our yard," said Katie.

"I know." Mama smiled, very gratified to find that her own estimate of the young man was the same as Clovelly's. Definitely not the marrying kind. Here today, and on his way tomorrow. After he had gone, Katie would break her heart for the space of about three sad sunrises, and then she would blossom like the proverbial rose. The proverbial rose—what a pretty thought that was! Mama sighed sweetly and turned to Bartholomew. "You must ask Katie to keep you company in the yard, my dear boy. She'll be very helpful."

184

On a less rounded face, Katie's expression would have been a gawp. Surely Mama realized that her future son-in-law was standing before her, but, instead of protesting the very thought of matrimony, she was apparently pushing ` her daughter straight into it. Katie took this as an omen, a promise that the path ahead of her would now run very smooth. Her heart sang, and the room shimmered.

Mama's gaze lingered upon her for a moment, then she said, "Run along, the two of you." As soon as they had gone out together, she bent to pick up the custard dish from the floor. Bartholomew, with the cat, had cleaned it out thoroughly, and, though Mama dearly loved a good trencherman, she felt a faint disappointment. Licking the tip of one finger, she dipped it instead into the sugar bowl and was restored. She then settled down to what remained of the honey.

Curled close to her feet, under the kitchen table, green eyes shuttered, rich in memories of cream and honey, the white cat slept, not as a boarder but in quiet possession.

For seven days, no cloud crossed the sun in its clear blue sky; leaves glittered green and gold, moon was conspicuous. Where Bartholomew went, Katie went too, and her face reflected at every minute the jubilee in her heart. With her usual instant conviction, she knew that Bartholomew would soon say, "Katie, will you marry me?" and she would answer, "Yes, Bartholomew." The knot would be tied forever. It was a vision to delight every clergyman in the world, and she could already feel upon her brow the patriarchal blessing of Noah, falling as gently as the wings of his dove.

On the morning of the eighth day, however, she woke suddenly out of a dark dream in which Bartholomew had left her, his whistle growing fainter down a long dark road and a fog rolling in behind him. In the dream, she had been running after him, screaming for him to stop, and he had not even turned his head.

She sat bolt upright, her mouth still open in the scream, her hands clutching her pillow as if it was the one that was leaving her. Then she hurled it across the room, sprang out of bed and ran to the window, willing the sky to be blue, the sun to be gold, and Bartholomew to be standing in the yard below her. . . . The sky was leaden, the sun was lost in gray clouds, and Bartholomew was nowhere.

She leaned over the sill, but all she could see was a world that was deaf and dull, trees hunched under the weight of their leaves, a road sodden with wetness and mud.

Then she gave a cry. Far up the road, in the face of such a day, in the rain and the mud, there was a man walking. She could see him only dimly, but she could make out the independent set of his shoulders, the lively back, the easy walk that was not quite a swagger.

Plain as disaster, it was Bartholomew Morgan, and the dream was true.

Katie did not stop to think; it was not a moment for thinking. Snatching up the white shawl that had travelled with her, she flew down the back stairs and out into the yard, down the path and onto the road. She was fleet of foot and fleet of mind, and, as she ran, she tried terribly hard to think of even one good reason why Bartholomew would be on the road at such an hour and on such a day.

There were no good reasons at all, and her heart, knowing the worst, told her that Bartholomew was abandoning her forever. She began to cry, and the bright tears ran down her cheeks and got lost in the weeping weather, but she only sniffed angrily and ran faster, crying his name like a mewing seagull.

When he heard her, he turned completely around, and, understandably, he stared. Katie was already damper than he was, being more diaphanously clad and wearing, besides her nightgown and her shawl, an added dampness of misery that was very pervasive.

He reached her in three steps, took her by the shoulders, and gave her a slight shake.

It was not so much the shake that returned Katie to her senses, as it was the way he stared at her. She had a sudden vision of herself through his eyes—her shawl a matted mess, her hair plastered across her face, her voice wailing like a screech-owl.

"Katie!" Bartholomew said, and let her go.

Her chin quivered. She raised it piteously, wanting him to cup it in his hand and lift her wet face to his. After a moment, she said tearfully, "I th-thought you were going away. I thought you were going away without even telling me."

He, thereupon, cupped her chin in his hand and lifted her wet face to his. "I'm not going away. If I were going away," he said lightly, "I would have taken my cat with me."

She was dying of anguish, and he was mocking her. Unversed in love, she felt only the storm that it made. She slapped his hand down, and she stood there, glaring now, hot enough to dry the clouds. "I don't care if you do go," she said furiously. "And it's not your cat!"

"Yes, she is."

"No, she isn't! You stole her!"

"I did not," said Bartholomew, between his teeth, "steal her."

"You did. You stole her."

"I did not steal her." For a moment he was glaring back, and then he said suddenly, "You shouldn't be standing there like that. You'll catch your death of cold."

"I never catch cold," said Katie, as haughtily as possible. "And, if I do, it's not your business."

"No shoes."

"I never wear shoes," said Katie.

"A little thin shawl," he said.

"It's wool," said Katie, "and very warm." She pulled it tight around her.

"A nightgown made of nothing at all."

She tried to pull the nightgown too, but it was like wet tissue and there was a faint sound as of something ripping. She grabbed at it. "Go away. We'll send your cat after you."

He laughed, and she was more furious than ever. The green eyes had dangerous gold lights. "I told you," he said, "that I wasn't going away. Can't a man take a walk on a wet morning without your thinking he's leaving forever?"

"I don't care if you do leave forever!" She yelled it at him.

"Well," he said, "there's that, of course," and, without any warning at all, he picked her up in his arms.

She was too startled even to shriek, and to tell the truth she was not of any mind to do so. Her anger ran out at her toes. She sighed richly. She curled herself into the warmth and delight of Bartholomew's arms, and instinct caused her to snuggle. Improving on instinct, she put one arm around his neck. Experimentally, she breathed his name into his ear.

"You're sopping wet," he said matter-of-factly, then he

hoisted her a bit higher in his arms and struck out for home. All the way back, she hugged him tight.

Mama, standing at her bedroom window and thinking her morning thoughts of Cornelius (which were different from her evening thoughts, but markedly interesting), saw Bartholomew striding toward the house, with the rain wet on his dark hair and carrying what appeared to be a stray lamb or a sack of potatoes or a human form.

When he got close enough, she was able to identify the very human form as her youngest and most contrary-minded daughter, arms wrapped firmly around Bartholo-mew's neck and head tucked firmly under his chin. Mama breathed her approving "At last!" Katie's tumbled look could not have been more reassuring to a mother's anxious heart. It must have been a beautiful night.

Pulling on her rose-colored dressing gown and tying it most casually, she pattered down to welcome the wan-derers just as they came through the kitchen door. "My loves!" she said cordially.

Katie raised her head, opened her eyes and closed her softly parted lips. Very lingeringly, she slid out of the arms that held her and stood, tipsily upright, in the mid-dle of the floor, smiling at nothing.

The ruffles of Mama's bosom heaved with satisfaction. Between herself and Katie, the kitchen now seemed to have acquired a somewhat voluptuous look of its own, a slight swaying of the walls, a divine softness of the floor, a cluttering of cherubs on the ceiling.

Bartholomew shook his head hard, said to Katie, "Get into something dry," scooped up the white cat from under the table, and left abruptly by the back door. It was a cruel thing to do to a cat, one would have thought, but the cat simply transformed itself into a white velvet cushion under his arm and let itself be carried away, purring regally.

"He's very sudden," Mama remarked, addressing no one.

"M'mm." Katie closed her eyes and tasted his suddenness.

She's far gone, thought her mother fondly.

"Mama—"

"Yes, my love." Mama leaned forward, and the front of the rose-colored dressing gown almost gave up its unequal struggle.

"Mama," said Katie, "I love him."

"Of course you do," her mother said warmly. "It's only right."

They stood there, gazing at each other in complete misunderstanding, floating gently on a tide of sentiment, breathing the golden air of the kitchen.

"Oh," said Katie at last, "it's so wonderful."

"Yes," said Mama, very soft-eyed and remembering, "it certainly is."

Twenty-two ∽

As far as Katie was concerned, the thing was done.

Having been carried home, wet with rain and limp with love, she now looked upon Bartholomew as her own. A proposal of marriage was the merest formality, and her posture was eager and receptive. She lived in his pocket. If his hand was free, she tucked her own inside it; if he bent over a bit of whittling, she was there to catch the shavings in her skirt; if he stroked the white cat, she stroked it too, making sure that their fingers tangled. If he took so much as a step outside the backyard, she was at his side and matching her step to his.

And Bartholomew seemed happy to have it so. His hand found hers as often as hers found his. Sometimes, he curled it into his palm, or traced the lifeline with infinite care.

Sometimes, he moved his fingers up to make a bracelet around her wrist. Then she would hold very still, while the bracelet slid higher, clasping her rounded forearm, and she waited for the words that he was supposed to say.

He did not say them, and she went on waiting. With him, she was perpetually on tiptoe. Away from him, she drooped, as if her petals were curving downward and turning pale at their edges for lack of water and sunlight.

Cornelius Porter, arriving after banking hours and before dinner-at-home, happened to glance up as he crossed the Thorne yard and was mildly surprised to see a frieze of three figures on the rooftop, outlined against a modest sunset. One was Bartholomew, one was Katie, and the third was the white cat. They had a certain wild charm, and he mentioned this to Mama in a spirit of appreciation and curiosity.

Mama explained. "They're putting back the shingles that the last storm blew off. It was Clovelly's suggestion. And I must say," she said, "that it was very sweet of her, because she loves putting on shingles. Clovelly can be very selfless." She followed him into the front room and into their usual chair, which was large enough for two persons if they were friendly.

"Katie looked happy enough," Cornelius said judiciously, "as far as one can tell anything about a person on a roof."

"She's not happy. She mopes. At least, she does when Bartholomew isn't around. I cannot tell you," Mama said, very emphatically, "how shocked I was when she told me that *nothing* had happened, the morning he brought her home so wet. Nothing! It was really very deceitful of her, Cornelius. I have never seen a young girl so radiant."

"I'm sure she didn't mean to deceive you."

"I suppose not. She's a dear child at heart, but she's certainly odd. And," she noted, a bit testily, "she is certainly not getting anywhere."

"Where," said the banker cautiously, "is she trying to get?"

"She's still trying to *marry* him," Mama said, "and it's all your fault. You gave her your blessing, and it's caused a great deal of confusion."

"It is *not* my fault," said Cornelius, sounding defensive, "and it was you who caused the confusion. You distinctly told me that the child had forsworn marriage."

"That's what she told us. I was *so* pleased."

"—and then she said the forswearing was only temporary, and I must say she made it all seem very reasonable."

Mama said, "She gets that from me," and smiled.

He let it pass, not feeling quite up to coordinating Mama and reason. "I mean, she made marriage sound reasonable."

Mama tapped her foot and said "Yes?"

"Well, there you are," said Cornelius in triumph. "There you are. There's nothing I can do, even if . . ."

But she had started her sentence before he could finish his. "She still thinks he intends to marry her, you know, and he won't. He's simply not the marrying kind."

"How do you know?"

"Well, one can see it at a glance. In fact, it's the first thing my girls noticed about him, and I agreed absolutely."

"That's a very arbitrary decision you've all made," Cornelius said severely. "A *female* decision. It's perfectly possible that your Bartholomew's intentions are completely honorable."

"Oh, Cornelius!" She sighed the ostentatious sigh of a patient woman.

He mumbled something conciliatory, aware that there

193

was apt to be no meeting of minds on this subject, and also aware that he was in no position to judge marital ties. He was certainly devoted to his dear wife and family, and he would not have had things changed, but on the other hand—He shook his head and looked distressed.

Mama understood at once. It was the banker in him, and she loved the banker because she loved Cornelius. "Dearest," she said, patting his hand, "I think you really ought to have another of your little chats again."

Cornelius looked even more distressed. "I will *not* talk to Katie. She muddles me."

"It's not Katie I want you to talk to. It's Bartholomew."

"You mean," Cornelius said palely, "that I should ask Bartholomew his intentions?"

"Exactly." Mama smiled up at him. "Then he'll tell you that he has no intentions about marrying Katie, or anyone else for that matter. And then you can tell Katie, and then Katie—"

"Yes, precisely," Cornelius said indignantly. "And then Katie, our poor little Katie—What then?"

"Then Katie can get on with it," Mama said, somewhat crassly. "And high time, too."

"Never!" said Cornelius.

Mama said serenely, "Oh, but of course she will."

"I don't mean she won't get on with it," he said hastily. "I only mean that—Good God, my love, you do put the most unsuitable interpretations on everything!"

"Then what did you mean by saying 'Never'?" She sat up very straight. "I am only asking in order to be informed."

He could not fail to observe the faint chill in the air, but he was determined to state his position in a precise manner. "I mean that I will not ask that young man what his intentions are toward Katie."

"Oh," said Mama.

"Never," Cornelius repeated, just in case she had got things wrong again.

"May I have a word with you, young man?" said Cornelius Porter.

Bartholomew turned back from wherever he was going and said, "Certainly" with great politeness.

It's his eyebrows, Cornelius thought uneasily, or perhaps it's his chin. Not quite piratical, but not a clubman's either. Would he make a suitable husband? Probably not. But then would Katie make a suitable wife? He cleared his throat and said "Er-ah-uh," as if it was all one word.

"Sir?" said Bartholomew, voice and eyebrows not matching.

Really, this was a difficult fellow. Cornelius rocked on his toes for a moment, trying to regain his corporate identity, trying to imagine the lad on the other side of a broad mahogany desk, respectfully applying for a loan. . . . He cleared his throat again. "Any dependents?"

"Sir?"

"Do you have any wives? Children?"

Bartholomew said, "No. No dependents, unless you count the cat."

"I do *not* count the cat." Hearing his voice rise, Cornelius tried again. "Are you planning any?"

"Cats?"

"Wives!" said Cornelius desperately.

Bartholomew shook his head.

"I mean, a wife," said Cornelius, floundering.

Bartholomew shook his head.

A sound financier never retreats. Cornelius said, "I believe in marriage," and he reverted to rocking on his toes once more, though less securely.

195

Bartholomew nodded. "Some do."

Cornelius pounced like a tiger. "But you don't."

"No," Bartholomew said mildly. "It ties a person down." There was quite a long pause. Cornelius ceased to rock. "Sir?"

"Yes?" said Cornelius eagerly.

"Was there anything else you wanted to ask me?"

Frankly, no. Cornelius shook his head. Bartholomew gave him a quick look, then turned on his heel and left the room. His shoulders back view were rather like his eyebrows; one did not quite know what they meant.

Cornelius stared after him uneasily. Certainly the young man was not the kind of whippersnapper to whom one would give a loan. . . . He contemplated the word *whippersnapper* and substituted *bandit,* but that did not quite fit either. Nothing really fit the young fellow.

Fellow was the word; loans were not made to fellows. Cornelius began to feel better, once more a man of sound judgment, representing his client's best interests. Breathing quite normally once more and eager to notify his client that he had worked everything out, he went to find her. "No problem at all," he reported heartily. "That young fellow has no intention of marrying."

Mama said that was wonderful.

"He says it ties a person down."

"Just what we've been telling Katie," Mama approved. "And here is Katie now."

Here she is, indeed! thought Cornelius, and getting prettier every day.

"Tell her," Mama ordered.

"Tell her what?" said Cornelius.

"Tell her you've been talking to Bartholomew."

"*Tell* me," said Katie quickly. Just the mention of his name, and she looked like a sky full of stars.

196

Cornelius was suddenly terrified. He had known all along that he ought not to meddle . . . But he had not been meddling, he had only been trying to oblige his heart's love. . . . Never try to oblige your heart's love. . . . His mouth opened, closed.

"Tell me," Katie demanded. She was not pretty, she was beautiful.

Damn Noah! Damn Noah and his Ark and his wife and his tribe. What right had the Bible to put such thoughts into a young girl's head? "I wash my hands of the whole business," Cornelius said fiercely, at the top of his voice, and he stalked belligerently out of the room, like the coward he was, pausing only to say over his shoulder, "You tell her!"

So Mama told her.

Katie heard her out, in such an intense silence that even Mama felt it and her voice trailed away. "So you see . . ."

"No," said Katie, "I don't see."

Her mother made a small sound, half cluck, half sigh. Katie looked at her gravely. "I am going to marry Bartholomew," she said.

"But, my darling, you can't marry him if he won't marry you," Mama protested, adding with unusual logic, "It takes two to make a marriage."

"I'll change his mind."

Mama said, "My dearest child, men don't use their minds when they get married."

"Then," said Katie, reckless and calm, "I'll change his heart."

Twenty-three &

Less than an hour later, Katie sought out Clovelly and found her doing nothing in the kitchen. Katie joined her and, for a few minutes, they did nothing together.

Then, casual as a passing leaf, Katie said, "Clovelly, dear. If you should see Bartholomew looking for his cat to-night—"

"Yes?" said Clovelly.

"—would you mind just telling him that you saw it go into my bedroom?"

Clovelly was silent for a full second. When she spoke, her voice was as pure as a crystal bell. "Katie my love," she said, "I shall be delighted to inform Bartholomew of your message." One would have thought that she had just received a gift of exceptional merit and charm. Her eyes were as luminous as stars, and so were Katie's. Dreamy and enchanted, the two sisters looked at each other for a long time.

At last! thought Clovelly.

At last! thought Katie. She turned and floated gently away.

Clovelly gazed after her, smiling, and it was a smile that combined deep satisfaction with a very sincere respect. Then she nodded to herself and floated off in the opposite direction, eager to spread the happy news that Katie had finally come to her senses.

The knock at the door coincided with midnight.

Either by good fortune or natural endowments, Katie (who, up to now, had been circling the room like a frantic June-bug or a moth at a candle) had just contrived, after the ninth try, to arrange herself on the bed in a pose as comfortable as it was graceful. The pose took full advantage of the moon, which was trailing its long white fingers through the window, and equal advantage of her long white nightgown, which was her best one and had lace bestowed all across its front.

Beside her, in the crook of her arm, purring deeply, lay the white cat.

The cat had been the unknown quantity in Katie's plan, but it had behaved beautifully, letting itself be scooped from its favorite chair, bundled into a basket, rushed off to a strange room. Now, when the knock came, it merely lifted its head and stared briefly, then closed its green eyes and went back to the lullaby purr.

Katie shifted slightly on one rounded elbow and said "Come in," with some difficulty in her breathing.

"It's me," said the door.

"Who?" said Katie to the door, knowing very well but wanting to hear.

"Me. Bartholomew."

"Oh." She had not quite allowed for the sensation of tumult, but she did manage to keep her curves moderately composed. "Oh, come in."

From the other side, out there in that dreadfully draughty hall, Bartholomew said, "I only wanted to know if my cat was in there with you."

"Cat?"

"Yes. Cat." He did not sound very patient.

On sudden impulse, she sat up straight, gathered the cat and the pillow into her arms, leaned over the edge of the bed, and stuffed them beneath it. There was a soft growl, but that was all. She maneuvered herself back into what she hoped was her original pose, and was pleased to find that, this time, it was even more flowing.

"No," said Katie, responding to that disembodied and beloved voice from the hallway. "No cat. At least, I don't think so. . . ." She let her voice trail away.

"Clovelly said—"

Dear, dependable Sister Clovelly. Dear, dependable white cat. There were no more growls from under the bed, and it seemed such a favorable omen that she almost began to enjoy herself.

"Katie?"

"Yes, Bartholomew."

"I asked you about my cat." A faint gritting of teeth beyond the threshold.

Katie shrugged a shoulder, so warm and white and nicely displayed that it seemed a pity no one was there to see it. "Well, come in," she said, managing to sound hospitable, managing not to trip over the catch that persisted

200

in her breathing. "Come in, Bartholomew. The door's not locked." She pulled the sheet a little higher.

The doorknob turned, and Bartholomew came into her bedroom, looking like a thunderstorm.

What he saw, of course, was what he was meant to see. A cloud of dark hair, sea-water green eyes, white hands clutching white sheet, round white shoulders. A quickening of breath and pulse, a sudden tempest in the lace, a trembling, a stir.

What Katie saw was her destined mate, standing like a young tree, a lance, an arrow. If she had been less taken up with her own breathing, she could have credited herself with several well-chosen similes, but the most she could do was to swallow hard and to lick her lips with the tip of her pink tongue.

They were both silent for the space of, say, seven heartbeats.

Then, "My cat," said Bartholomew woodenly.

She swallowed again, made a gesture with the fingers of her right hand—limited enough to keep a grip on the sheet, but wide enough to include the whole room. "I—I don't think it's in here," she said, "but you're welcome to look."

He seemed to have some difficulty in tearing his eyes away from her, and her self-assurance began to creep back. Her grip on the sheet relaxed somewhat, and she even managed a gracious nod of her head.

Bartholomew said, "Thank you." He stood looking around the room for a moment, and then he made a small noise, such as one cat might make to another in a friendly situation. There was an underbed scuffle of paws, softer than dust, and the white cat marched out. It looked regal and attentive.

"My goodness!" said Katie, astounded at having a cat in her bedroom. The stumble had left her tongue, and the lace of her gown was no longer in such tumult. She waited, watching him.

"Katie—"

She waited a moment longer, and then she said, "Yes, Bartholomew?" The cat mewed and jumped to his shoulder, and he brushed it off. Katie smiled. There was no longer any question who came first in his heart. "Yes, Bartholomew?" she said again.

He was taking forever about it. He was hers, and she loved him. She wanted to help him, to be a mate, to be a helpmate. He was not the first man to stand tongue-tied in front of her, but he was truly the only one she had ever longed to hear speak.

The cat, banished, crossed the room and jumped to the windowsill, where it sat and mewed again, very softly, to the moon, to the trees, and to the silver mice just outside.

"Katie—" Bartholomew said again, hopelessly unoriginal.

Oh, my love! cried Katie's heart, and it would not wait an instant longer. She slipped out of her bed and ran to him on bare feet, coming so close that, if he moved at all, she would be in his arms. She turned her face up and waited for the words—the same ones that the Mooncalf had uttered when he had never intended to utter them at all—Katie, I love you, Katie, will you marry me?

Bartholomew said nothing. He simply pulled her into his arms as he had pulled her that wet, wet day on the road, and he lifted her off her feet. Then, carrying her as if she weighed nothing at all, he started across the room toward the bed.

Now, he would say the longed-for words.

He would say them *now*.

He would say them . . .

He did not drop her onto the bed, he pushed her there, and she tumbled backwards like a doll in a hayfield.

From the windowsill, the white cat gave a howl in the moonlight, and Katie cried out "No!" Then she put her two hands against Bartholomew's chest, and she shoved him away from her with all her strength.

He did not stagger and fall flat, like Eben Swann, but he did loosen his hold for just a second. In that second, she broke free.

He caught at her shoulders. "Katie—"

"No! No! No!"

"Katie—"

"Go away!" Katie shouted from inside the Ark.

His hands dropped to his sides. He turned and strode out of the room, and the cat leaped from the sill and streaked after him like white lightning. The door slammed.

Katie threw herself on the bed and burst into wild tears.

Twenty-four ✑

"I don't pretend to understand it," Clovelly said. *"All I know is* that she threw him out of her room."

"The cat, too?" said Octavia.

"The cat, too."

The sigh of four was as the sigh of one. Mama said unhopefully, "Do you think I should have another talk with Cornelius?" but the silence was unanimous. Cornelius, though loyal, had not been all that competent.

They stood and looked at each other, soft-eyed gold, amber, and sapphire, and then Octavia unknit her brow. "Dawn, couldn't you tell Katie that you made a mistake about Noah, that he and his wife weren't really married?"

Dawn pushed back a lock of hair that had fallen across

204

her brow from worrying. "I'm afraid not. It's all written down in the Bible, you know."

"Lots of things are written down that aren't true."

Mama said reprovingly, "I hope not, dear," and then added, "Although everyone knows that the Holy Bible is full of traps."

"Traps?" said Clovelly.   .

"Well—snares."

Momentarily, they were all in danger of being side-tracked, but the forces of motherhood and sisterhood dragged them back to the main issue. Clovelly went on. "We have to do something. The poor child has been crying in her room all morning.—One could talk to Bartholomew, I suppose, but what could one say?"

No one offered to talk to Bartholomew, and Clovelly nodded agreement with their silence. "Well, I suppose someone could talk to Katie. . . ."

Dawn said, "You're the oldest, darling," and Clovelly did not dispute the point, which, in view of Mama's presence, was patently disputable. "But I don't *want* to talk to Katie," she objected, and then, "Do you think I could make her see reason?"

"You could try."

She drew a deep breath, straightened her shoulders, and thrust out her chin, accentuating one of the prettiest jaw-lines since Eve. "Very well. If it's my duty, I'll do it."

"Clovelly!" said Mama, pained.

Clovelly, already on her way, paused to comfort her mother with a light kiss on her ruffled brow. "Never mind, darling. I'll do it out of pure affection, if that makes you feel better." She looked at the three of them, all so worried, then added "Damn Noah," with considerable feeling, and departed on her reluctant mission.

Katie's door was shut tight. Behind it, there was nothing but silence, stony even at a distance.

Clovelly raised her hand to knock, found the formality altogether ridiculous, turned the doorknob and walked in. Katie was sitting on the side of her bed, still in her nightgown, bare feet on the floor, arms folded, green eyes staring straight ahead. When her sister crossed the room and touched her shoulder, the statue did not move.

"Katie, love—" Clovelly said, in a voice to charm a bee off a honeysuckle.

Katie said icily, "I have no privacy."

Clovelly smothered exasperation. "Do you want me to go away?"

Katie shrugged, but at the same time she was not able to suppress a very small sob, and Clovelly stayed. She stood for a moment, looking down at the dark hair that was so tangled from having been wept in, then she moved away and began to wander around the room, touching things aimlessly. The mirror on the far wall caught her as she crossed its oval. "Katie—" She picked up a small box, put it down. "Katie, I'm sorry it didn't work out."

"What didn't work out?" said Katie through tight lips.

"Telling Bartholomew that the cat was in your room."

"It wasn't your fault," said Katie with terrible politeness.

Clovelly, agreeing mentally with Mama that duty was an overrated virtue, sighed heavily, but the sigh had no effect. She crossed the room once more (stamping softly) and sat down on the bed, leaving a space between them. "You haven't had any breakfast," she said.

"I don't want any."

"Nor lunch."

"Thank you, Clovelly. I don't want any lunch."

"Mama's very anxious about you, dear. We all are."

"There's no need to trouble yourselves."

"Oh, Katie, really! Do stop being such an idiot!" She regretted her outburst instantly, she who had planned to be so wise and kind. She said lamely that she was sorry and then she sat, scowling at her clumsiness and beginning to feel that she might just as well get up and go away— Send another sister, send Mr. Porter, send the cat, send Bartholomew . . . Oh, if she only could!

Experimenting, Clovelly tried the name *Bartholomew* aloud, and then repeated it with a question mark— "Bartholomew?"

There was a stillness, and then a small, bereft voice answered her. "Clovelly, he hates me."

"Oh, he couldn't!"

"I threw him out."

"Yes, I know."

"Do you know why?"

"Well, I suppose," said Clovelly, with really marvelous delicacy, "that he—made advances."

Katie nodded forlornly. "I thought he was going to ask me to marry him. I *knew* he was going to ask me to marry him."

"Darling," said Clovelly, "a man who is making advances is simply not in a fit state to propose marriage. And, to tell you the truth," she added dreamily, "a man proposing marriage is usually not in a fit state to make advances.—Do you love him, Katie?"

The green eyes turned on her, holding such an intense light that she caught her breath. Then Katie said, "But he hates me now," and the light went out. Clovelly pulled her sister's head down on her shoulder and heard her say something else, inaudible.

"What?"

"I said, I'll never see him again."

"Of course you will, child." Clovelly stroked the long, tangled hair with long, straight fingers. "All you have to do is comb out these snarls, and throw cold water on your face, and go downstairs and find him. Then you say, 'Bartholomew, I love you,' and he'll forget that you ever threw him out last night."

"Will he ask me to marry him?"

The silence was thunderous.

Finally, "You see?" said Katie, and raised her head.

They stared at each other without moving, and then Clovelly gave a small wail. "Katie, I don't understand you at all. Ever since Dawn told you that stupid story about that wretched Noah—"

"It's not a stupid story," Katie said sadly. "Not to me, anyway. Ever since I heard it, I've known it was what I wanted." If her eyes had been brimming with tears, Clovelly might have known how to answer, but they were dark emeralds, not sea-deeps. "I can't help being me, Clovelly."

Struck by this undeniable truth, Clovelly sat quite still. "Katie," she said at last, "may I ask you a question. Do you plan to be—" Her voice brushed the word like a moth's wing—"faithful?"

"I haven't thought about that," Katie said, and there was a pause during which she did so. Then, "Yes," she said. "I guess I do."

Clovelly stood up. Her hands were clasped loosely in front of her, her chin was slightly raised, her eyes very level. The oval mirror caught her once more, and she nodded back at her own image, grateful to see someone she understood and who understood her. Then she reached out one finger and touched, very gently, the cheek of her incomprehensible sister. "You're very—odd," she said.

Katie nodded, without raising her head, and Clovelly turned and left the room. After all, there was nothing more that anyone could do.

Twenty-five ✑

The mirror which had given Clovelly back as a portrait now gave
Katie back as a smudged sketch, red-eyed and weary from
weeping, red-nosed and dismal. Her hair was not so much
in snarls as in tatters, and even the lace on her nightgown
sagged.

She stared at her reflection, thinking miserably that it
was no wonder that nobody wanted to marry her. Seeing
this woebegone creature, the Mooncalf would never have
fallen on his knees, Timothy would never have folded her
into his arms alongside the kitchen sink, Joseph would
never have woven a single strand of poetry. Even the
swaggering Eben Swann would have rejected her without a
second glance.

She rubbed her knuckles in her eyes and turned away from the mirror. "Someone will marry me," she said unsteadily, wanting the sound of any voice in the very empty room. Not Bartholomew, whose name was now a dagger, but *someone*. There was no law that said husbands and wives had to love each other; only mates needed to do that. If Emma was here, she would say that all Katie had to do was to find anyone who was willing, and to forget Bartholomew.

No more Bartholomew, no more Bartholomew ever again.

Katie lifted her heavy hands and ran her fingers through her hair, and then, suddenly, fiercely, she began to braid it. One long braid, hanging neat and forever down her back, instead of a cloud of dark silk spread on a pillow . . .

Her hands dropped. Her body went slack as if it might slide off the edge of the bed, fall to the floor. She sat there, without moving, looking straight ahead and not seeing anything at all.

When the white cat put its paw in at the door, asking to enter but entering anyway without being asked, Katie did not turn. It waited briefly to be acknowledged, and then, used to attention, it meowed.

Katie's chin jerked up, and she said "Go away!" almost angrily. She willed it to disappear, not to sit staring at her in her own room, belonging to Bartholomew, meowing about him. "Go away," she said again, and, being a cat, it came to her immediately and rubbed against her ankles.

"Go away," she begged, "please go away," and then she gave a sudden and very sad little cry and gathered the cat up into her arms. She put her forehead down on the soft white fur, and she held it against her so tightly that it struggled, and then she held it even tighter. Whether it wanted to stay with her or not, it was something of his and she could not let it go.

"Oh, Bartholomew, oh, Bartholomew," she whispered and began to rock back and forth, trying very hard not to cry, muffling his name in the cat's silk and snow softness. It gave up trying to escape and surrendered to her grasp. The beginning of a purr made a faint rumble in its throat.

From the doorway, Bartholomew said, "I've come for my cat."

Katie stopped rocking and sat perfectly still.

When he came into the room and closed the door behind him, she got to her feet and, making herself stand very straight, she held the cat out to him, wordlessly, at arm's length. It hung from her hands like a bundle of white rags, four paws dangling foolishly, heavy and limp from nose-tip to tail.

Everything was just as it had been on the first day they met—herself holding the cat and staring over it, and himself standing in front of her, eyes daring and lively and fastened on her face.

She knew very well how her face must look to him now, a misery reflection of her head, stuffed and silly with woe, but she managed to lift her chin. She had not wanted to see Bartholomew ever again, because there was nothing for them to say to each other any more. It was for the sake of his white cat that he had come into her room for the last time. The cat was the only thing he cared about.

"Take it," Katie said stonily.

He hesitated a moment, then he shrugged and reached out. The cat instantly gathered itself back into cat-shape, stiff-legged, spread-clawed, before it bounded free and dropped lightly to the floor, rid of them both. It arched its back, stretched elegantly, sat down on the rug and started to wash, beginning with the plume tail and working slowly and with perfect concentration.

Deserted by her small rampart, Katie did not move.

There was a widening silence until Bartholomew said "Katie" and took a step toward her. She closed her eyes, telling herself that, when she opened them, he would be gone.

She opened them, and he was still there, staring at her, a long look as if he was committing her to memory. She turned her head away from him and fixed her eyes on the floor. All that she asked now was for him to go as quickly as possible, to leave her alone. He had only to pick up his white cat and carry it with him to the door. The door would open, and the door would close. . . .

A long shiver went all the way through her. At last, and so much too late, she had learned the real truth about Noah. It was not that the world was meant to go in pairs, tidily, two by two. The real truth about Noah was that he had never been in love.

She waited, holding herself very tight, in one piece, for fear that she might break into a million.

Bartholomew said "Katie," and he put his hands on her shoulders. She tried to move away, but there was no strength in her at all. She swayed, and he pulled her into his arms, holding her close against him. His mouth came down on hers. Her knees buckled, her arms went limp, her whole body felt as if it was made of cotton—of silk—satin—cloth of gold . . .

"Katie, my darling," said Bartholomew.

"Yes," said Katie hopelessly. There was nothing left any more of her vow to marry. There was nothing left of her.

"Katie, my darling," said Bartholomew, "will you marry me?"

Katie fainted.

And, somewhere in Noah's heaven, Noah's dove sighted land.

Epilogue ❧

One day, of course, they all left Falling Grove, as Cornelius
Porter had always known they would—Mama, Clovelly,
Dawn, Octavia; Katie with a wedding ring on her left
hand and that hand held in Bartholomew's; the white cat,
soft, self-sufficient, beautiful.

The town was busy growing into the city it had always
pretended to be, and the house stood empty for less than
two months. The town's leading banker was able to nego-
tiate a very favorable contract for its sale, and he quietly
locked up in his desk drawer the dear and useless piece of
paper that Mama had signed.

Since he had never really left his own world, Cornelius
was able to return to it without comment. He grew a little

stouter perhaps, his waistcoat was tighter, he seldom twirled his hat.

Only, sometimes, his wife Addie would find him sitting in his armchair, eyes closed, smiling quietly. "It's done him good," she would think, and then she would leave him entirely alone and go back to her own particular garden of flowers, knowing, as she had always known, that not everyone in the world wants the same thing.

The End